RAINY DAYS IN UPPER BAMTON

UPPER BAMTON BOOK 2

※

BETH RAIN

Copyright © 2022 by Beth Rain

Rainy Days In Upper Bamton (Upper Bamton Book 2)

First Publication: 31st July, 2022

All rights reserved.

No part of this book may be reproduced in any form or by any electronic or mechanical means, including information storage and retrieval systems. Except for use in any review, the reproduction or utilization of this work, in whole or in part, in any form by any electronic, mechanical or other means now known or hereafter invented, is forbidden without the written permission of the publisher.

Published by Beth Rain. The author may be contacted by email on bethrainauthor@gmail.com

※ Created with Vellum

CHAPTER 1

'Nope. Noooope! I *really* don't like you, you know!'

It was fair to say that Patricia Woodley didn't like her new bicycle. In fact, as she wobbled along the rain-soaked, rutted riverside path on her way back to her cottage in Bamton Ford, she'd go so far as to say that she *loathed* her new bicycle.

Every time she tried to find the correct gear lever in amongst all the other gizmos and do-hickeys that crowded the handlebars, something went very wrong. It was a miracle she hadn't landed in the hedge yet… but there was still time.

'Stupid… effing… will you just do what I tell you to?!'

There was one glaring problem with this idiot contraption – it wasn't anything like her old bicycle. Wally had been perfect. Simple, elegant… and more than a little bit battered around the edges. She hadn't minded that though - he'd always got her safely from A to B.

Unfortunately, Wally had also turned into a travelling rust-heap and over the past six months had started to shed vital parts. In the end, with many regretful tears, she'd had to retire him and buy herself an upgrade.

Upgrade, shmupgrade...

As she didn't have a car, she'd reluctantly forked out an extortionate amount for this thing. She hadn't given it a name yet, and she wasn't really sure she was going to bother with one either. That honour was reserved for things she actually liked. But this thing was soulless. To say that it hadn't been love at first sight was the understatement of the century.

There were *plenty* of other problems with this ridiculous, new-fangled, over-engineered travesty besides the fact that it wasn't Wally. For a start, Patricia didn't like the narrow, uncomfortable seat that tried to cut her in half every time she needed to nip out for a quick bit of shopping. The last time she'd headed over to Upper Bamton vineyard for *Knit One Pour One*, she'd not been able to sit down again for the whole evening!

Patricia despised the level of clutter on the handlebars too. She couldn't work out the point of half the levers, knobs and thingamajigs that controlled the gears or – in her case - didn't!

She wasn't stupid though - she realised she was

probably just using everything wrong. A lot more practise and she'd get the hang of it... maybe. But that just made her hate the bike even more. She didn't *want* to practise on it!

Right now, though, she didn't have a choice. She needed to get back to her cottage before the dark, threatening cloud that had been hanging over the valley all morning decided to dump its contents on her head. She'd never known such a wet summer! It was late July already, but it had rained every single day for weeks on end. The fields were sodden and the dark green canopy of oaks that shaded the riverside path spent their entire time dripping. It was days like today that made her wish that she'd bothered to learn how to drive.

Patricia twiddled with one of the levers, hoping it was the right one. The ominous clunking sound that followed and the fact that she now felt like she was trying to pedal with a herd of elephants tethered to the bike made her pretty certain she'd got the wrong gear. Again.

'I really hate you, you know?' she muttered, flicking the lever wildly until she could move her legs again. It would be the last straw if the chain decided to fall off... though that would be pretty typical of the way things were going at the moment. The last couple of weeks had been one disaster after another.

Clonk.

Finally - a gear that didn't feel like a total catastrophe. Who needed this many gears anyway? Wally didn't have gears. If you wanted to go faster, you just had to pedal harder. Yes, he'd been ancient and lacking in some of the features of the more modern bikes… okay, *all* the features… but that had been completely fine with her. He'd had two wheels, a seat… and that was about it. The brakes had been shot to pieces - you could just about slow down enough to hop off if you really clamped your hand around the lever for the back brake. Other than that, he'd been perfect. Who needed two brakes anyway?

The best thing about Wally had been the wicker basket that strapped on behind the seat. Patricia knew that it was quite unusual to have the basket at the back, but she'd loved it. It had been perfect for loading everything up – wool, needles, shopping… she'd even been able to stash her coat in it when she was out and about and got too warm. No matter what she'd thrown in there, Wally had always felt safe and secure and remarkably well balanced.

The same could *not* be said for this thing. The new bike didn't have a basket. That's why she'd been forced to wear her oversized raincoat with all the pockets so that she could stash her shopping in them on the way home. Patricia sighed. She was going to be forced to buy a hideous backpack or something like that, wasn't she?

Urgh – she just wanted Wally back. She felt like she

was in mourning for an old friend. He'd been simple – and she liked simplicity.

Patricia knew that she was a bit of a walking contradiction when it came to that. Most people considered her job as a professional knitwear designer to be fiddly and complex and anything but simple. She guessed that, in some ways, they were right. The patterns she designed were technical – tricky to pull off if you didn't understand the language of knits and purls, slips and skips.

If she was ever asked *how* it all made sense to her, she liked to compare it to mathematicians. They could look at a complex formula without seeing a bunch of tangled brain-spaghetti. They saw both the problem and the solution all lined up in front of them, as clear as day. It was the same with her and knitting patterns.

Patricia had never had a problem deciphering the rules of wool and needles. Before she was even able to master the ins and outs of English grammar, she'd been able to look at a knitting pattern and instead of seeing lines of indecipherable code, she'd see a finished piece of knitwear. It was a language that simply made sense to her.

What Patricia liked about knitting best was that you either got it right - or you didn't. There was nothing ambiguous about it – it was pretty obvious if you got something wrong.

Knot.

Hole.

Tangle.

Patricia cursed as she hit a stone and the bike swerved dangerously on the muddy track. She really needed to concentrate if she was going to make it to the end of the path and arrive home safely!

Her cottage stood right next to the river separated from the water by a gorgeous little back garden and a scruffy bit of river bank that also belonged to her.

Technically, this track actually led all the way *into* the river. A little way beyond her garden gate, it turned into the slipway that was used by the Bamton Ford ferry over the summer months. Not so far this year, though. James, the young guy who usually captained the boat was a bit busy with his newborn daughter, and the boat itself was still sitting upside-down on her stretch of the riverbank awaiting some TLC before being pressed back into action.

Patricia let out a sigh of relief as she caught the first few flashes of the white, wooden garden fence ahead of her through the trees. She was nearly home. Patricia adored her riverside cottage... life was usually pretty peaceful there. At least, it had been until her recent bout of stress and bad luck.

It felt like the early summer had served her up one problem after another - as if the universe was determined to rock her smooth sailing through life. First, Wally had given up the ghost and then, just last week, the water tank in the roof above her spare room had randomly decided to leak. That had been a real disaster.

She used her spare room as a studio - and the water that had cascaded through the plasterboard ceilings had ruined the majority of her knitting pattern collection – both her carefully sourced vintage finds and her own hand-written designs. This would have been a disaster any time, but as she was currently on the tightest deadline of her career to date, the loss had brought her to her knees. The temptation to admit defeat was very real and something she was still debating. Giving up really wasn't in her nature... but she wasn't sure if she had much choice in the matter this time around.

It didn't help that no one else was taking the loss all that seriously. She'd had to physically restrain herself when one of her neighbours had commented cheerfully that "at least nothing important had been damaged... after all, they *were* just knitting patterns."

Patricia had a sneaking suspicion that the same neighbour wasn't too sad about the demise of Wally, either... mainly due to the fact that she'd attached a fantastic old brass horn to his handlebars. It had been seriously loud. Give a good honk on that thing, and people certainly got out of your way - and she'd rather enjoyed using it on that particular neighbour a few times over the years!

Patricia let out a huge sigh and continued to make her ungainly way down the gentle slope towards her cottage. There was definitely something off about the balance of this thing. Maybe it was just too heavy compared to Wally…

Her garden gate had just appeared ahead of her when Patricia's stormy mood took a definite turn for the worse. There was a stranger on the riverbank beyond her garden. On *her* stretch of the river bank in fact.

She didn't recognise his face, and Patricia knew practically everyone in Upper Bamton. After all, the place wasn't very big, and Bamton Ford was even smaller – just a little collection of houses that had been a part of the same country estate. The stranger seemed to be taking a great deal of interest in the Bamton Ford ferry. She felt a sense of unease creep up her spine and she shifted slightly on the seat.

The bike promptly wobbled again and Patricia let out a huff. She really should be paying more attention to the path rather than eyeballing the stranger – but she couldn't help it.

Out of habit, Patricia reached out to give a good honk on the horn to get his attention – only to realise that it wasn't there because this wasn't Wally.

Damnit!

Patricia sucked in a breath as her angry, jerky arm movement threw her off balance again and sent her careening across the muddy track.

Argh! She was going to come off if she wasn't careful!

With her heart rate ramping up several notches, Patricia forced the handlebars back in the right direction, simultaneously squeezed her hands around both brakes… and started to slide.

Suddenly, everything was happening in slow-motion. Both tyres had stopped turning, but her momentum combined with the slick mud meant that she was sliding straight past her garden gate. She could only imagine that the bewildered expression on her face was probably pretty comical by this point – but she was a very long way from laughing.

Beneath her, the lane turned into the slipway for the ferry – slick with green slime and disuse.

Oh no…

OH NO!

She was heading straight for the river and there was absolutely no point veering either way – it was too late for that. Any second now and she was going to get an exceptionally chilly dunking in the deep, swirling waters of the Bamton.

'Aaaaaaahhhhhhh!'

A very un-Patricia-like squeal left her lips and she closed her eyes tight - as if that might protect her from what was about to happen.

Any moment now...

And then… nothing.

Patricia opened her eyes again, only to find that she was mere feet from the drop into the water, and a stranger's arms were wrapped firmly around her. The bike was still underneath her, but it had partially slumped onto the slipway in a Victorian-style swoon.

Patricia swallowed, trying to get her bearings. The first thing she noticed as her senses began to recover was that the arms around her were wearing a nicely worked navy-blue sweater. At a guess, she imagined that it was probably knitted using Blue Faced Leicester – soft and luxurious.

The next thing she noticed was that the stranger she'd spotted fiddling around with the ferry was smiling down at her. And he had an extremely nice smile. One you could get lost in… one that extended from his mouth all the way up to his eyes, where little wrinkles fanned out in a friendly fashion from their hazel-green depths.

The third thing she noticed was that he didn't seem to want to let her go – though her befuddled brain knew that this was probably because he was doing his best to keep her upright and stop her from tumbling the last few feet into the river.

Suddenly affronted, Patricia straightened her spine. Every fibre of her being stiffened as shock and a good dollop of mortification coursed through her.

'Do you mind?!' she said, her voice cold and haughty.

The man promptly let her go, taking a step away from her and holding his palms up in an apologetic gesture.

Huh. It was amazing how badly you could behave

when you were embarrassed, wasn't it? But now she'd started down that route, Patricia decided that it would be best to maintain her air of indignance.

So *what* that he'd just saved her from a good dunking?

So *what* that she was already missing the warmth coming off his lovely jumper. It really did look rather wonderful on him… just right in fact!

Patricia gave herself a shake.

Pull yourself together, woman!

The hero-act and a nice jumper didn't change the fact that this stranger shouldn't be there at all. This was private property, and he had no right!

CHAPTER 2

Patricia glowered into the stranger's face, trying to get her head on straight. Something about his slow smile and kind, crinkling eyes was making it incredibly difficult for her to catch her breath, let alone figure out which way was up.

'You okay?' asked the man. His face was full of concern, but he clearly wasn't going to dare to make a move back towards her in case she bit his head off again. In fact – he was looking at her like she was some kind of injured, wild animal... rather than an idiot he'd just saved from a soggy plunge into the Bamton.

A low growl started to form at the back of her throat and Patricia struggled to keep it in. Maybe this guy wasn't quite so far from the mark with the whole *wild animal* thing after all.

That look he was giving her was doing nothing to improve her mood. She felt more shaken than her near-tumble into the river warranted – but she refused point-blank to admit that it might have anything to do with this random stranger who'd come to her aid. She could still feel the echo of his strong arms wrapped around her - cased in a soft jumper that really was rather beautifully made, now she came to look at it properly.

Patricia wasn't really in the habit of losing her temper... except under dire circumstances like when a ball of wool ran out at a crucial point in a pattern and the next one's dye-lot simply didn't match, no matter what the label said. Or when there was a knot in the yarn. Why did that always happen right on the chest, so that the piece instantly gained an unwanted little nipple-lump?! Knitting disasters aside though, she'd describe herself as fairly level-headed. Chilled, even.

That wasn't the case right now, though. She'd most definitely lost her chill – big time! Her horrible ride on the new-fangled bicycle from hell might have started things off on the wrong note, but standing in front of this stranger having made a total idiot out of herself... well, the wrong note had developed into a full-blown disaster symphony.

The man was looking at her with some concern now – clearly waiting for her to speak and prove that there wasn't something seriously wrong with her.

Say something, idiot! Anything!

Every muscle in Patricia's body tensed even further. She felt all twisted up like a human pretzel. She couldn't get any words to form around the lump in her throat.

As far as she could tell, she had three options – she could start crying (tempting but mortifying), have a good giggle (undignified and possibly uncontrollable) or lose her rag completely (not pretty but extremely satisfying).

Whichever one she chose, she needed to do so quickly before the mad boiling sensation inside her made her explode. Maybe she was losing the plot…? It was a strong possibility.

Patricia started to nod slowly, still completely dumb as she tried to force her body out of its weird stupor. Stupid man… if only he'd just wander off and let her gather her thoughts rather than staring at her like she might go feral at any moment.

If she was being fair, it wasn't really his fault, was it? Even if she wasn't about to admit it out loud, it was pure embarrassment that had her all twisted up like this.

Even though the guy had backed away a few more paces, his eyes were still fixed on her. To add to her definite discomfort, Patricia felt herself start to blush - the wave of heat beginning somewhere in her muddy boots and sweeping right up over her head. She raised her hand to swipe loose strands of hair off her face… only to make contact with something woolly.

Nooooooo!

Wasn't it bad enough that she'd just made a

complete prat out of herself and nearly hurtled headlong into the river in front of this man? It seemed not. Patricia had completely forgotten that she was wearing the most ridiculous hat ever to grace a pair of knitting needles.

It was a classic Marjorie Binmore creation, knitted just for her – and she hadn't had the heart to turn it down. Her fellow *Knit One Pour One* member had proudly proclaimed that she'd created it using an unravelled sock, an old cardigan and a pair of original 1980s legwarmers. Patricia guessed that last one would account for the lurid neon green stripes… and perhaps the repurposed sock might explain the rather unique smell that it never seemed to lose, no matter how many times she washed it. Considering all that, it fitted beautifully – which was why she'd forgotten it was on her head in the first place.

It had been the nearest thing to hand as she'd dashed out of the house earlier, hoping to get to town and back again in between the showers. Fat chance! And now, as she stood damp and dishevelled in front of this man, wishing that for once she was wearing something a bit sexier than scruffy, mud-spattered jeans and an oversized, slightly smelly raincoat… the hat was the last straw.

Patricia let out a huff, acutely aware that she was still being stared at. By this point, he was probably preparing to call the emergency services for the lunatic in front of him.

Why did she have to be dressed like a slightly soggy bag-lady? Especially when this guy was just… just… so annoyingly gorgeous?

Today was just going from bad to worse. Maybe she should just put her tail between her legs and disappear into her house without saying anything at all. She could slink back to bed and pretend none of this had ever happened.

But no – that wasn't really her style either. So what that she looked like a half-drowned scarecrow? She wasn't up for playing the damsel in distress right now.

Sucking in a steadying breath, she narrowed her eyes and glared at the stranger.

'You're on private property, you know?' she said, finding her voice at last.

Her words were icy cold, and she kept her spine stiff and straight as she did her best to haul the stupid bike up out of its dead faint without losing her footing on the slimy slipway.

'I know,' the man replied calmly.

A little too calmly for Patricia's liking. Was it her imagination or was he being altogether a bit too smug? Fine… she'd show him!

'That's the Bamton Ferry you're *interfering* with. It's council property. You shouldn't be fiddling around with it without their permission.'

'Yes – I know that too,' he said, giving her that slow smile of his again. 'I wasn't exactly interfering with it, you know… I was just looking.'

Patricia bristled. As if *that* was any kind of an explanation for trespassing on private property!

'Well, you shouldn't be,' she grumbled. 'I let them store it here over winter so that I can keep an eye on it. I take that job seriously, you know. It's had to stay here a bit longer this year, that's all. But if you think you can just turn up and nick it, you've got another thing coming.'

She paused, breathing hard as she stared back at him. A little twitch was going in his cheek and he looked very much like he was trying not to laugh in her face. It just served to ramp her irritation up into a blazing, white-hot anger. Here came that rage she'd been promising herself!

'I've seen you now,' she said, her voice low and quivering slightly with unspent emotion. 'I'll report you to the council if anything goes missing.'

'I'm not planning on stealing anything,' the man said mildly. 'Let's start again. My name's Harry.' He paused and stuck out a large hand.

Patricia stared at it in surprise. It was nice... clean, not grubby... tidy nails... she tended to notice little details like that – she couldn't help it - they mattered to her.

Still, she wouldn't shake this *Harry's* hand. So what if he'd just given her his name... it could be a fake, couldn't it? Even if it wasn't, she still had no idea who he was. It didn't change anything. Besides – it didn't matter who he was – he still shouldn't be hanging around on her stretch of the river bank.

So she just stood there, propping up the dreadful bicycle, wearing the worst clothes she owned, and waiting for him to give her a better explanation.

It took several long seconds before Harry got the message and dropped his hand with a shrug.

Good. Somehow Patricia had a feeling that it wouldn't be safe for her to touch him again. If she did, she couldn't be held responsible for her actions!

'My son James usually operates the ferry,' said Harry, his voice deliberately light. 'But his wife has just had a baby. Now - I love my boy dearly, but this is his first kiddie – and he's not exactly a realist. He thought he'd be able to carry on with life exactly as it was before the little wriggler was born, without making a single change.'

He paused and smiled at Patricia, but she forced her face to remain stony. Harry sighed and continued.

'Turns out the ferry's one step too far. I've got a feeling his wife might have put her foot down! Anyway – James had already made a commitment to the council, and he's already late getting it up and running this year as it is – and it has to be back in the water in time for the Bamton Abbey Open Day - so he asked me if I'd do it for him.'

'Oh, he did, huh?' said Patricia. She wasn't entirely sure why she was arguing with such a reasonable explanation, but frankly… it was just that kind of day.

'Yep!' said Harry, clearly taking the fact that she'd engaged with him at all as a good sign. 'Cheeky blighter said I wasn't doing very much and the exercise would do me good!' Harry paused again and grinned, patting his stomach through the luxurious jumper. 'Anyway – I thought I'd come down and check what I was about to let myself in for before agreeing to anything. I wouldn't want to let anyone down by saying yes and then backing out at the last minute.'

'So you thought you'd just randomly let yourself through the gate and-'

'I did knock on your door to introduce myself first,' said Harry, cutting her off, 'but you were out. James did say it would be a good idea for me to say hello before I started to move anything around... I guess he was right!'

Patricia huffed as Harry raised his eyebrows. He was clearly waiting for her to back down, laugh it all off and let him get on with whatever he'd been doing when he'd had to drop everything and come to her rescue. For reasons unknown to the logical, nice part of her personality, Patricia found that her bubbling rage had different plans. So she just stood there and stared at him.

'You can call James if you like,' said Harry. 'He'll vouch for me. Might be a bit cheeky about it at first... he's like that and, to be honest, he seems to be getting worse with the sleep deprivation... the little missy is leading them a merry dance at the moment... but I promise you he'll say who I am… eventually!'

'Hmm, we'll see about that,' muttered Patricia.

She cringed inwardly. At some point during this ridiculous exchange, she seemed to have abandoned all attempts at being a normal human being and was now channelling a pantomime villain. It wasn't a part that suited her at all… but it was a bit late now to switch to playing the princess. She had a feeling that would just make him think she was an even bigger weirdo.

Ah well – she'd already hit rock bottom. It was time to retreat before she started drilling into the granite!

Without another word, Patricia scooted her stupid bike around in a wide circle and headed back up the slope towards her cottage, being careful not to slip in the slime. A faceplant right now would just about put the finishing touches to her awful morning… though, no doubt this Harry bloke would probably quite enjoy watching it happen after the way she'd just treated him.

Reaching the relative safety of her garden gate, Patricia glanced back down towards Harry only to lock eyes with him again. He gave her a cheery little wave of his hand, then turned away to continue his inspection of the upturned boat. Unfortunately, he didn't move quite fast enough to hide the quirk of a smile that was playing around his lips.

Patricia let out a long growl of frustration as she pushed the bike down her garden path and let herself into her hallway. She leant the bike up against the wall – something she'd promised herself that she'd never do because who wanted scuff marks on the paintwork and tyre marks on the floor? But right now, that was the least of her worries.

Bloody man.

Bloody bike.

Bloody river.

She turned to the full-length mirror that hung on the hall wall and let out a low, horrified groan. It was even worse than she'd been expecting. Bag lady didn't even begin to cover the damp, drowned-rat look she had going on.

She snatched the hat off her head and threw it on the stairs. She was going to bury that thing deep in a drawer, never to be seen again.

CHAPTER 3

'It's official - you're an idiot!' muttered Patricia as she scrunched up the lemon-yellow sun dress and lobbed it over her shoulder. Reaching back into the wardrobe, she yanked a green and white striped shirt from its hanger with a clatter.

Holding it up in front of her, she glared at herself in the mirror on the back of the open wardrobe door. Nope – definitely not. In fact, she wasn't even sure why she had this shirt in the first place. It quickly followed the dress, landing on top of the towering heap of clothes on the bed behind her.

The discard pile was getting out of hand… as was Patricia's bad mood. The problem was - she knew she'd come across as a total raving lunatic in front of that Harry bloke just now - and the knowledge that she'd behaved so badly was just serving to make her crankier than ever.

What that had to do with her burrowing to the back of her wardrobe on some kind of fruitless mission for something sexy and sophisticated to wear, however, was beyond her! She had no clue what had gotten into her – but she wished she could snap out of it!

It didn't normally take her this long to get changed out of her cycling gear. Usually, she'd just grab a shower and then throw on the nearest, slouchiest ensemble she could find. Comfortable old jeans, an ancient cotton man's shirt and a big, soft jumper tended to be the order of the day.

Usual didn't seem to apply to today though. She'd been standing here in just her bra and knickers for what felt like ages as she'd excavated the entire contents of her wardrobe.

Patricia shivered as a cold draft tickled her skin, causing goose-bumps to rise on her bare arms. It might be nearing the end of July, but it was far too chilly here in her rickety old cottage to be standing around in front of her cupboard wearing nothing but her undies.

Slamming the wardrobe doors closed, she turned back to her bed, intent on donning the first thing that came to hand.

'Shit!' she squeaked and promptly dropped to the floor. 'Aw no no no!'

The bedroom curtains were wide open. That meant that anyone out on the river bank would have had a full and unadulterated view of her in her undercrackers. In this case, *anyone* just happened to be her twinkly-eyed saviour. It seemed that she was destined to make the biggest prat out of herself as possible in front of this guy!

Gah! Now what was she going to do?
Maybe he hadn't seen her?
Fat chance...

Her bedroom window looked straight out across the river and the little stretch of bank where the ferry sat. She didn't usually have to worry about people being able to see in here. Other than the two days a year when James turned up – once in the springtime to collect the ferry and then once in the autumn to tuck it up again for the winter months - no one ever went out there. The ferry's route across the river itself was just out of view – so Patricia had always been safe from prying eyes... until now!

How long had she been standing around in her undies? For all she knew, Harry could have been watching her the whole time as she'd undressed and pranced around the bedroom on full naked display!

Well, she certainly couldn't stay crouched down here on the carpet, could she? Besides... it was cold and she was starting to feel like a first-class plonker.

Keeping herself low to the ground, Patricia started a semi-naked commando crawl towards the window. When she was close enough, she scooted around and pressed her back against the wall underneath the sill. Stretching her arms wide, she reached out to either side of her and grabbed the edges of the curtains.

With one swift movement, she yanked them closed then let out an irritated huff as they swirled around her head.

Patricia struggled out from behind the heavy drapes, spitting loose strands of hair out of her mouth. Smooth!

Making sure she hadn't managed to leave a gap that would showcase her wobbly bits all over again, Patricia clambered back to her feet.

Her heart was thumping traitorously against her rib cage. She *had* to know if he'd seen her or not. Unable to stop herself, she pressed one eye right up to the join between the two curtains and, easing them open just the tiniest crack, peered down at Harry.

He had his back to her, and he was bent low over the boat, completely engrossed in whatever he was doing. Her heart sank.

Oh honestly, woman!

Patricia wanted to kick her own backside as a jolt of disappointment ran through her. Given that Harry was facing away from the cottage, it was pretty clear that he'd managed to miss the inadvertent peep show she'd just tried to treat him to.

She should be relieved. What was *wrong* with her?!

'Clothes!' huffed Patricia, letting go of the curtains and striding back to the bed. She needed to stop behaving like a hormonal teenager – moody baggage one second, and … well… whatever *this* was the next.

Right. She needed to find something nice to wear. If

she was going to have to face him again, she wanted to at least make sure that she looked good…

'Get a grip!' she hissed at herself.

She was being completely absurd! Why the hell should she be worrying about what this Harry bloke thought of what she looked like – in her clothes, or out of them for that matter?! He'd already seen her at her worst and most bedraggled, hadn't he? Anything would be an improvement after that!

Patricia grabbed a pair of tatty old jeans and yanked them on, followed by an ancient white cotton shirt and her favourite Arran jumper. It was too big for her by miles - and completely delicious in its shapelessness.

There. That was better. She already felt a bit more like herself. She'd leave putting the clothes mountain back in the wardrobe until later - right now she had a more pressing matter to attend to. She needed to check out that this *Harry* person was who he said he was.

Patricia made her way back downstairs towards the kitchen where her old-fashioned landline hung on the wall. She'd been too focused on changing out of her slightly damp and ridiculously unflattering ensemble when she'd first come indoors to call James straight away. But now… well, now she needed to check that the man with the twinkly eyes was safe to have roaming around on her stretch of riverbank… though, if she was being honest, the only weird nutter out there just now had been her.

She didn't really know why she'd been such a snidey

cow-bag with Harry. After all, she knew James - his *supposed* son - pretty well. James had been operating the little passenger ferry for several years now… maybe as many as five – she couldn't remember. Either way, she liked the guy. They never exactly spent *that much* time together, but when she did chat with him on one of her rare crossings over the river, he was always polite, a little bit cheeky, and incredibly grateful to her for permission to stash the ferry on her section of riverbank.

James only ran the ferry during the summer months when there were plenty of tourists pottering around and wanting to take a ride across the river. They liked to go for day trips over to the ruins of Bamton Abbey on the other side. Other than that, most of the passengers were either locals or archaeology tutors and their students from the local university travelling to their long-running dig site at the Abbey.

Usually, James's season would have already been up and running for weeks by now. He usually started making crossings at the weekends during the Easter holidays, building up to working seven days a week by this point in the year.

Patricia sighed as she grabbed James's number from underneath its little boat-shaped magnet on the front of the fridge. Should she call him? Maybe she was being ridiculous… why on earth would Harry pretend to be James's dad anyway? That would just be weird!

Besides, he knew so much about James that it had to be true... didn't it?

James and his wife Mattie had indeed welcomed a little girl not too long ago. In fact, she'd even knitted some tiny garments for the newborn. She'd expected to be able to hand them over to James when he'd returned to his ferry duties – but he hadn't appeared, and Patricia hadn't wanted to bother the young couple while they were learning to navigate such a whopping life-change!

It was a shame, though – she had quite a stack of bonnets, cardigans and even blankets – all knitted to her own designs and ready for the little mite to start wearing. She'd made several different sizes, but if she didn't get a wiggle on and hand them over soon the baby would have grown out of the smallest ones already!

Perhaps... if Harry really *was* James's dad... maybe she could hand them over to him instead? That was a normal-person thing to do, right? After all - that would make him the baby's grandad...

'Grandad?!' she said out loud in surprise. Blimey, Harry definitely didn't *look* like a grandad... he was all handsome and rugged, and had a lovely taste in jumpers and...

Patricia shook her head. How exactly was this conversation going to go anyway?

Yeah... hi! It's Patricia... there's a guy here who knows everything about you and might be trying to steal the ferry...

or he might be your dad... or maybe the nicest knight-in-shining-cashmere axe-murderer I've ever met. Either way, he saved me from falling in the river and I think I fancy him because I was a total bitch. Oh... he is your dad? Great... carry on then!

Okay. That decided it. She was *not* going to bother James with her insane babbling today!

Instead, she ambled back out into the hallway and headed for the cupboard where she'd stashed the bundle of baby clothes. Opening the door, she took out the paper-wrapped package and peeped inside. Yes – there they were – all soft lemons, whites and peachy pinks – perfect for the new arrival.

She took it back through to the kitchen and placed it carefully on the scrubbed pine table. Running her fingers over the soft weave of the alphabet blanket right at the top, Patricia stood for a moment, trying to decide the best course of action.

Urgh. If she was going to be near neighbours with Harry while he fixed up the ferry right outside her cottage, and then operated it for the rest of the summer, she was going to have to apologise, wasn't she? After all, he *had* saved her from getting soaked, and she'd been pretty short with him. Actually, if she was being honest with herself, she'd been downright unfriendly.

'Patricia Woodley, you're an idiot,' she muttered, hurrying to fill the kettle and peeping out of the window as she did so.

Yup – there he was, still fiddling around under the tarpaulin. She quickly replaced the kettle and flicked the switch to set it boiling. Then she stared down at her clothes. Maybe she *should* change again?

'Even bigger idiot,' she laughed, shaking her head.

If Harry was going to be around all summer, she couldn't go through some kind of silly performance with her clothes every time there was a chance he might catch a glimpse of her, could she? Harry was bound to see her in her normal uniform of scruffy jeans and ancient, slouchy jumper before too long, anyway.

Besides, what did it matter?! If he was someone who went for high heels and dresses… well, then they were totally incompatible anyway. Not that she needed them to be compatible. She wasn't thinking about that… but…

'Oh, shut up brain!'

She'd make two cups of coffee and head back out there to mend some fences. It was the least she could do. Perhaps she should find a couple of biscuits to take with her too - after all, she *had* been pretty foul.

Reaching up into one of the high corner cupboards, Patricia rummaged through her chocolate supply. Ah ha! Chocolate hobnobs should do the trick. They'd strike the correct, apologetic tone.

She placed two onto a pretty, vintage plate - where they proceeded to look incredibly sad and lonely. She added two more, her guts tying themselves in knots as she wondered what kind of message it might send if she took too few out... or too many come to that...

'Now you're just being daft!' she huffed, emptying the rest of the pack onto the plate. Good grief! Since when had she become quite such a neurotic mess? Oh right – since an entire tank of water had ruined months and months of work. That had done the trick nicely!

Patricia's stomach squirmed with worry. How on earth was she going to be able to re-do all that work in time for the deadline? She hated not being in control like this. Maybe she should just cancel the job entirely and tell her potential buyers that she was going to have to let them down. There were bound to be some pretty horrid repercussions if she did that... but what other option did she have?

Patricia let out a sigh as the kettle came to the boil. First things first – she had an apology to make.

CHAPTER 4

It was a bit of a juggling act to make it safely down onto the riverbank bearing both mugs of coffee as well as the plate of biscuits. Patricia came very close to emptying the entire lot onto muddy grass more than once. She should have just left the blasted biscuits in the packet – that would have made things a bit easier. She didn't know what she was trying to prove – she *never* put biscuits on a plate. What next? Was she going to start adding paper doilies to everything?!

Sticking her tongue firmly between her teeth, she forced herself to concentrate as she made her way over the soggy, slippery grass towards the boat.

Harry was so focused on the patch of peeling, wooden hull that he'd uncovered from the tarpaulin, that he clearly hadn't noticed her appearance. Patricia drew to a standstill and stood quietly for a moment, watching him, willing him to turn around. That said, she was quite enjoying the view from this angle if she was being honest. Maybe a couple more minutes of uninterrupted ogling wouldn't be the worst thing that had happened to her this morning!

Sadly, the heat from the two mugs she had grasped precariously in one hand was getting too much for her poor fingers to take. Damn it... now she'd noticed it, it was getting positively scorching!

'I brought you a peace offering,' she blurted.

Harry turned to her, and she felt a swoop in her stomach as that slow smile lit up his face again.

'Coffee,' she added. 'It's... quite hot.'

Taking the hint, Harry made his way quickly over to her and, with some difficulty, managed to take one of the mugs from her without spilling a drop.

'Thanks,' he said, raising it to her as if it was a glass of champagne, then taking an appreciative sip.

'Yeah, well, I'm sorry I was rude earlier,' she said, pulling a face. She felt pretty foolish all of a sudden, standing there with her coffee and the stupid plate of biscuits. 'I promise I'm not usually like that. I'm just having a bad day... week...'

She stopped and shrugged. It would feel a bit melodramatic to add "month... life..." to the list. Also, in the grand scheme of things, that wasn't strictly true – it just felt like it today.

'It's okay,' said Harry, thrusting his free hand into his pocket. 'I figured that might be the case. Mind you, your day would have been considerably worse if you had ended up in the river.'

Patricia nodded. 'Yeah,' she said awkwardly. 'Thanks for that, by the way.'

Harry shrugged and sipped his coffee again. Not knowing what else to say, Patricia did the same, still awkwardly clutching the plate of biscuits in front of her.

'So, you're the lady with the bicycle…' said Harry, then he smirked. 'Sorry… that's, erm… that's pretty obvious, I guess.'

Patricia smiled at him tightly. It seemed that he was just as uncomfortable around her as she was with him.

'All I mean is - James told me about you,' he said, his cheeks now slightly flushed. 'You get to ride the ferry for free for letting us keep the boat here out of season.'

'That's right,' she said, nodding. She glanced down at the plate in her hand. 'Biscuit? They're chocolate ones…'

Harry shook his head. 'Thanks, but I'm trying to watch my weight.'

'Why?!' said Patricia without thinking. Then she promptly shut her mouth and bit her tongue as his eyebrows shot up in amusement. She hadn't been able to help it though - he looked pretty perfect to her… but then, what would she know? She'd been on her own for so long that she'd clearly forgotten how to behave like a normal human being, let alone being able to trust her ability to judge what was or wasn't attractive.

'Well,' laughed Harry, his dancing eyes resting on hers in the most unnerving manner, 'James keeps telling me I've piled on a few pounds since I stopped working. He likes to tease me about it because he's a total git! Anyway, I'm off the biscuits for now... the chocolate ones at least. Plain ones are fine... but I can't leave chocolate alone... the entire plate would be empty before you know it!'

'Oh,' said Patricia, not knowing what else to say.

'But, if I'm honest, I'd eat all the plain ones too... so I'm not going to lose anything off the waistband either way, am I?' he grinned.

Patricia's eyes strayed to his waistband, and she curled her toes in her boots. Despite his delicious, chunky jumper, to her eyes, it didn't look like Harry was carrying a single spare pound of flesh under there.

And now she was staring at his waistband. Great.

'What do you think? Do I need to lose a few pounds? Be honest!' chuckled Harry, clearly noticing that her eyes were glued pretty far south of his face.

Patricia's eyes flicked upwards and met his with horror. 'I... erm... I...' she stuttered.

'Sorry, I didn't mean to put you on the spot or anything,' laughed Harry.

He paused and they both stared at each other in silent amusement - or horror - Patricia couldn't figure out which one it was. Maybe she should have just stuck to her guns, stayed inside and let Harry think she was a totally nutty bitch-face all summer. That would probably have been more comfortable than what was happening right now, at least.

'Anyway, thanks for the coffee... and maybe I'll take just one as you've been so kind,' said Harry, giving her a cheeky wink and helping himself to a biscuit.

Patricia watched, her insides melting, as he popped it into his mouth whole and closed his eyes, chewing with a look of pure delight on his face.

Yep – she *definitely* should have stayed inside.

'I'll bring the mug back when I'm finished,' he said, making her jump slightly, realising that - yet again - she'd been caught in the act of staring at him. Before she could respond, Harry turned away and started mooching back towards the boat.

Patricia let out a long, slow breath. Right, that was her off the hook then, wasn't it? She could just go back inside now and get on with her day. She could pretend none of this had ever happened. She'd done her duty – she'd apologised, brought him coffee and made things... well... maybe not more comfortable between them, but at least not quite so openly stroppy.

The thing was, Patricia didn't particularly want to head back inside. That would mean she'd have to face real life in the shape of her looming deadline and her total lack of interest in doing any work towards it. What she'd much rather do right now was perch somewhere vaguely comfortable and watch Harry while he worked.

Why she'd want to do something so bizarre was

beyond her. After all, there wasn't anything remotely interesting about watching someone faffing around with the peeling bottom of an old boat, was there?!

A quiet voice nudged the back of her brain and suggested that maybe, just maybe, she needed to admit to herself that it was the person *doing* the faffing that she was interested in watching? But that would just be silly, wouldn't it?! She didn't know anything about this guy... other than the fact that he was a chocoholic and thought he was a bit overweight even though he very clearly wasn't...

A blast of chilly air blew down the river, whipping her hair around her face and shaking some sense into her. It was going to rain again at any moment. She'd leave Harry to get on with it and go back indoors out of the way. After all, she could just as easily see what was going on from her back windows, couldn't she? Plus, that would have the added bonus of keeping her nice and warm and out of the weather... and there would be much less chance that Harry would catch her while she was busy ogling him.

Even so... she really would like the chance to talk to him again before he disappeared...

'Baby clothes!' she said, making him turn in surprise.

'Eh?'

'Sorry, I was just thinking out loud,' she said with an embarrassed laugh. 'What I meant was - when you bring the mug back, would you mind knocking on the door? I've got a few things I knitted up for the baby - but I haven't seen James for ages now, so I haven't had the chance to hand them over.'

'That's really kind of you!' said Harry, treating her to yet another smile. Patricia had the uncomfortable sensation that she was already becoming addicted to those warm, slow moments of sunshine. 'Now that you mention it, I think James told me that you're a knitter. You went to that thing they held at the vineyard too, didn't you?'

Patricia nodded.

'James bought me some gorgeous bottles of wine while he was there… I should have known that he was buttering me up, ready to ask me to take this on,' he laughed, gesturing back to the boat. 'What was it called again? It had a great name…'

'Knit One Pour One!' said Patricia. 'I love it – Alice Merryfield started it… can't beat a bit of wine and knitting! Perfect combination… or, at least, it is at the beginning of the evening. It can lead to all sorts of exciting tangles and dropped stitches the later it gets!'

'I'll take your word for it,' said Harry. 'I can't knit for toffee… though I know my way around a decent glass of wine! Anyway, I reckon some new clothes for the little blighter will come in very handy. She's at that stage where the moment you change her into something clean, she's sick all over it… I remember James was the same as a baby.'

Patricia grimaced. Babies weren't really her forte.

Thank heavens she'd had the sense to knit everything in machine washable yarn though!

'Sorry... possibly too much information there,' laughed Harry. 'Mind you, things are easier these days with proper washing machines, aren't they? We didn't have one back when James was a nipper - couldn't afford one.'

Patricia's heart had just plummeted, and it took her a couple of seconds to figure out why. Then it hit her. It was the casual mention of "we". Of *course* Harry would be part of a "we" – after all, he had a son, didn't he?!

'Anyway,' said Harry, oblivious to her discomfort, 'I'll probably be another half an hour or so... I'd better get back to it.'

Patricia nodded. This time she took the hint and retreated back to the cottage without another word.

∼

Exactly twenty-five minutes later, there was a knock on the front door. Patricia forced herself to count slowly to ten before dashing to open it. She *might* have been loitering near the window, watching as Harry let himself through her little garden gate and made his way up to her door... but there was no way she wanted him to know that!

'Hi!' she said, beaming as she opened the door, only to be arrested by the kind, crinkling eyes again.

'Hey,' said Harry. 'Thanks again for the coffee. Here's your mug.'

Patricia took the proffered spotty crock out of his hands. She was planning to invite him in and maybe even get a bit more of a conversation going. She wasn't entirely sure why… other than the fact that she'd been loitering for a full twenty-five minutes, desperate to chat with this random stranger again. Now that he was standing right in front of her though, all her adulting skills – like being able to start conversations, and not dribbling over random men – seemed to have deserted her.

'You said you had some baby clothes?' Harry prompted.

Patricia nodded. 'Right. Yes - here…' she reached behind her for the parcel wrapped in paper - now tied with a pretty yellow ribbon. She hadn't been able to stop herself from tarting up the plain brown paper a bit.

'Lovely job,' said Harry. 'I'll be seeing them later and I'm sure they'll be thrilled to bits.'

'Thanks,' said Patricia. 'At least this way the little one will be able to get some use out of them before she gets too big!'

Harry nodded.

'Would you-' Patricia was about to ask Harry if he'd like to come in for another drink, but the huge dark cloud above her cottage chose that exact moment to do its thing. Rain started to fall, loud and insistent, and clearly intent on stopping their conversation in its tracks.

Harry shifted on the doorstep as a couple of large, wet splotches appeared on the paper package. He quickly tucked it up under his jumper.

'Don't want these getting wet,' he said. 'I'd better get going - I've taken up too much of your time today already.'

'Oh, okay,' said Patricia. Damnit - she should just ask him in - but the moment had already passed. Even as she debated it, the rain cranked up a notch.

'Catch you soon!' said Harry, raising a hand in hasty farewell as he ducked his head and dashed off to wherever he must have parked his car.

'Balls,' muttered Patricia, as she closed the door on yet another summer cloudburst.

CHAPTER 5

Patricia yawned widely and stretched her arms above her head as she stared out of her bedroom window at the leaden skies. She was absolutely exhausted. She hadn't slept well for several days now and she wasn't really sure why... or, at least, that's what she kept telling herself.

It certainly wasn't *anything* to do with Harry.

Perhaps it was the strange sense of waiting that had fallen over the cottage. That could definitely be the problem. It was like she was frozen. She was waiting for something, though what that *something* might be was anyone's guess!

Patricia sighed and raked her hands through her hair before twisting it into a messy plait over her shoulder. It wasn't really all that surprising that she was feeling discombobulated, was it? Not with the deadline drawing ever nearer. She was at a complete standstill, and she'd already had to postpone her meeting with Butter's creative team up in London once – she certainly couldn't do it a second time!

It was such a shame, really. When the opportunity had first landed in her inbox, she'd been thrilled. A bit scared too, of course, because she'd never worked with a big brand before, but it was the opportunity of a lifetime. This was the kind of thing that could take her career not just to the next level... but to an entirely new game played on a completely different board. This would see her collection of originally-designed woollies being distributed to gorgeous boutiques across the country. There had even been whispers of Paris and New York if things went well.

That had all been before the water tank had emptied itself through the ceiling of her studio, destroying months and months of hard work. Patricia felt a familiar drop of fear descend into her stomach.

In theory, she should be hard at work, re-working the designs, re-drawing the sketches that had been damaged, and sorting out the samples she was due to take to London with her. In reality, she hadn't touched the project since the tank had burst. It was like a big pause button had been pressed... the only problem was that she didn't know how to get going again.

Yep – there was no doubt about it – the situation was enough to make even the calmest and most collected of saints feel a bit antsy. She definitely wasn't a saint – but she was wound up like a watch spring.

Only… in her heart of hearts, Patricia knew this feeling didn't have anything to do with the water-tank disaster. She'd been more upset about the loss of her collection of vintage patterns than the work she'd put into the Butter project. She couldn't put a finger on it, but it had felt like some kind of relief when she'd discovered the big balloon of plaster dangling down from the ceiling and chalky, dusty water gushing all over her work in progress. That just wasn't normal, was it? She was probably just in shock. She just needed some decent sleep and she'd be back on track again.

Maybe she was coming down with a cold… or maybe she just needed more coffee… or maybe she was having too much coffee…

'Idiot,' she muttered, scanning the riverbank for what must have been the thousandth time in the last half an hour. Nope. Still no Harry to be seen. There was the ferry, sitting forlorn and upside down, waiting for some TLC… but there was no sign of life out there. She let out a sigh.

Bloody man. She should have known that he'd turn up, drop a mayhem-bomb inside her head and then disappear into thin air.

Maybe he'd decided that there was simply too much effort involved in getting the ferry back in the water for it to be worthwhile. Or maybe he'd come to the conclusion that working in such close proximity to her was too much bother… that was the more likely scenario after she'd behaved like such an arse the other day.

Well, whatever. She'd apologised, hadn't she? There wasn't anything else she could do. She certainly couldn't waste any more energy thinking about him... or checking whether he was out there every five seconds! If only she could force her subconscious mind to get the memo, then perhaps she could get back to some proper sleep again too! Because, if she was being honest with herself, Harry was the real root of her disturbed sleep.

The problem was that every time she closed her eyes, she would instantly fall into the same dream. It was becoming far too familiar. She was on her horrible new bike, slip-sliding towards a dark whirlpool when she was saved at the last moment... by Harry. But it wasn't exactly a pleasant dream - more like a nightmare where she woke with a jolt, her heart thumping in her chest and cold sweat prickling her forehead.

Patricia had no idea what her subconscious mind was up to - but she wished that it would quit it. She'd tried every trick she could think of over the past couple of nights, hoping they'd help her to drift off minus the mad dreams. Last night, in pure desperation, she'd decided that maybe her pillow was to blame, so she'd swapped it out for the spare she kept in the airing cupboard. It hadn't helped in the slightest.

Patricia turned to stare at her bed - part of her wishing she could just crawl back under the covers and hide... after all, the forecast for the rest of the day didn't look good. The rest of the week, come to that. The storms that were hurtling across the Atlantic towards them were promising heavy rain – or at the very least, some persistent showers. No one would care if she stayed in bed, would they? In fact, they probably wouldn't even notice. That was the joy of living alone. She'd get up again when the sun came out... and as there was no sign of the sun making an appearance any time soon, it looked like she was off the hook!

Patricia sighed. She remembered a long, rainy summer like this when she'd been a kid. Back then, she'd squirrelled a bunch of clothes airers, blankets and cushions to the old shed at the bottom of the garden and made herself a fort. She'd spent the entire summer holiday ensconced inside, listening to the rain beat against the tin roof while munching on sweets, working her way through a stack of Enid Blyton books and knitting squares for her very first patchwork blanket. It had been heaven. If only she could do the same now!

On a whim, Patricia strode out of her bedroom and threw open her airing cupboard. She might not be able to build herself a fort, but maybe she could make life a little bit more comfortable. The new pillow hadn't helped, but maybe a complete change of bedding would make it easier to sleep tonight... there wasn't anything quite like fresh bedding to send you off for a good sleep, was there?

She grabbed the brushed cotton, pastel striped set she'd bought because they reminded her of childhood, marched back to the bedroom and started to strip the old bedding off with gusto. At least it gave her something positive to do for a few minutes.

Patricia's eyes wandered over towards the window again. Nope. Still no one there.

'Bloody men,' she huffed, yanking off the old duvet cover and tossing it into the discard pile with a little more force than strictly necessary.

After a couple of minutes spent wrestling with the new cover, she was breathing hard and her hair had begun to escape from her plait. What the hell had she been thinking? This was a nightmare of a job even when she was in a good mood! No sooner had she managed to get one corner in the right position when the other one fell out.

'Gah! Just… get… in… there!' she huffed, shoving the entire duvet into the opening and giving the whole thing a rough shake. As *if* that was ever going to work!

Patricia promptly gave up and lobbed the entire thing back onto the bed, then turned to glance out of the window again.

It was like someone had flipped a switch. A lightbulb came on and her entire day brightened. Harry was back at last.

Patricia hurried to the window, careful to stand slightly to the side of the curtain so that she wasn't in view. Should she show herself and wave down to him?

There wasn't really any point – even if she was brave enough, the rain was coming down thick and fast, and Harry had his head bent low.

Patricia felt her mood sag briefly - then it sprang back up again as she watched him wandering around the ferry. At least he was here! She couldn't imagine what kind of work he'd be able to do out there today - it just didn't seem like the sort of day to do anything much outdoors somehow.

Maybe she should take him a coffee again… it was a fairly safe bet he'd need one. She could kick herself that she hadn't thought of making a cake. She'd been so aimless the last few days, at least it would have given her something to do while she was busy mooning around and pretending her deadline didn't exist.

Ah well. Maybe she wouldn't bother him after all. It was pretty unlikely that he'd want to stop and chat with her anyway. He was probably desperate to get the work done and get the ferry back in the water before he managed to miss the entire summer season. She'd get on with her day… and let him get on with his.

~

Patricia spent the next half an hour doing her best to avoid her bedroom window. She had better things to do than just stand there, gawping at Harry as he worked. Even so, she couldn't really help catching glimpses of him as she finished making her bed. Sure, it took three times longer than usual - but the window was just there, and where else was she supposed to look?!

Then, she discovered that her dressing table needed dusting and rearranging. She'd been meaning to do it forever – and now was as good a time as any. The fact that it stood right next to the window had absolutely nothing to do with it.

As she moved the duster in lazy, slightly pointless circles over the vanity mirror, Patricia noted that Harry had an interesting reaction to the rain. The drizzle that had been coming down steadily all morning had now ramped up a notch – the drops coming harder and heavier.

Rather than going to fetch a jacket like any normal human being, Harry stripped off his jumper and tossed it aside. It flumped down in a sodden heap in the mud, making Patricia cringe. She had to force herself not to rush straight out and save it from its grubby fate - and give Harry a lecture about looking after such a beautiful garment while she was at it. She just about managed to restrain herself, though. Harry probably already had her down as a complete nut-job after their first meeting, and she didn't want to cement the impression by launching a *Save The Woollies* campaign.

Despite Harry's careless disregard for precious knitwear, Patricia couldn't help but continue to stare at him in admiration. He was obviously one of those people who had no fear of getting soggy and cold. His white cotton tee-shirt was soon soaked through. Patricia swallowed. Hands-down, Harry would win any wet tee shirt competition going... especially if she was the judge!

She should go and do something... useful. Or at least, something less furtive than peering through the curtains like a little weirdo while the poor bloke was trying to work. She was just about to peel her eyes away when she suddenly found herself glued back to the scene unfolding below her.

'Oh my,' she mumbled. 'Oh *my!*'

Down on the riverbank, Harry had clearly had enough of being quite so wet. He'd suddenly come to a standstill and yanked the sodden cotton tee shirt over his head – revealing a beautifully brown, well-toned body.

Realising she was gawping at him like a stunned goldfish, Patricia promptly closed her mouth... but she couldn't take her eye off him. She didn't know what James was on about calling Harry overweight - there wasn't a single ounce of flesh out of place on the man. Considering he'd just become a granddad... Patricia shook her head slowly. She needed to get away from the window. It would be mortifying if he caught her watching him like this!

Still she didn't budge. She watched as Harry scrunched the tee shirt into a ball, the muscles in his arms jumping as he wrung a stream of rainwater out of the cotton.

Crikey – well – this was certainly one way to get warmed up on a chilly day! Hot and bothered would be closer to the mark! Patricia let out a sigh of disappointment as Harry shook the tee shirt out and pulled it back over his head. Damn.

Right. She needed to go and do something useful… like take a cold shower. Or maybe, if she stayed here long enough, he might do it again?

'Move!' she mumbled, forcing herself to take a step away from the window at last.

The show was over and she had work to do… but somehow, Patricia had a feeling that there might be a new scene in her dreams when she went to bed this evening!

CHAPTER 6

*R*ight, it was finally time to face the fact that she was staring down the barrel of a deadline. Considering most of the work she'd put into the project so far had been ruined, she really needed to get a wiggle on. This was no time to stand gawping at Harry while he was trying to work... not when she should be doing exactly the same thing.

Patricia pushed open the door of the spare room and let out a huge sigh as she leaned her entire weight on the wooden doorframe. She stared around the room, feeling her mood descend to an even lower low. She hadn't spent any time in here for several days now, other than to dash in and out to empty the industrial dehumidifiers she was running in an attempt to help the space dry out. Frankly, it was simply too heartbreaking.

Considering this had been a perfectly set-up studio

before the disastrous leak that had seen gallons of water pouring in from the roof space above - it was now a damp, smelly mess. The plaster that had been bulging from the ceiling in a weird, soggy balloon had now given up completely. Huge whitish-grey chunks of it had broken away and now littered the still-damp carpet underneath

Peeling herself away from the doorframe, Patricia tentatively approached one of the old trestle tables she'd set up in the corner. It had been a nightmarish job, laying out the sodden sheets of card and paper that had once been her vintage pattern collection. She'd been collecting them since she was a teenager. Now there was a good chance that - after almost three decades of carefully hoarding all that irreplaceable treasure - it had all been ruined in the blink of an eye... or rather - the burst of a pipe!

Still, she'd spread them out on an old sheet in the hope that some of them might be salvageable. The multi-page ones were probably going to be good for nothing other than the bin. Patricia had spotted that the minute she'd first attempted to peel the pages apart. It hadn't stopped her from painstakingly placing wodges of kitchen roll between the leaves in the vague hope that it might stop them from turning into papier mache as they dried out.

With a shaking hand, she picked up the nearest one – a beautiful 1940s wartime cardigan with the most exquisitely ribbed band - and instantly felt the tears spring to her eyes. It *had* dried out… but in doing so, it had gone wavy, crispy and rock solid. She tossed it back down onto the table, blinking furiously and willing herself not to burst into tears.

Maybe right now wasn't the time to face the rest of them… but then again, she needed to check over her own designs, didn't she? Otherwise, she'd have no idea how much work lay before her if she was going to meet this damned deadline.

She turned to the second table and sighed. This would teach her to handwrite her patterns like some kind of dinosaur. The ink had run on every single buckled, crinkling page. Some of them might be just about readable… but it would take some serious deciphering.

Patricia could curse herself – she'd been planning on taking the whole lot over to Upper Bamton vineyard so that she could scan them on Alice's machine. She hadn't thought there was any rush. If only she'd bothered to snap a photo of each page on her mobile - that would have been a huge help - but it simply wasn't her style. She was all about tangible things when it came to working on a project – sketchbooks, swatches and inked notes. All her patterns were handwritten and then amended by hand in tiny, squashed notes that now just looked like watercolour smudges on the ruined pages.

Luckily, she'd knitted most of the pattern parts up several times by this point. If push came to shove, she should be able to reverse engineer them - with a bit of focus and hard work. She hadn't actually sewn the final pieces together yet – which looked like it was going to turn into an unexpected bonus, rather than the worst case of procrastination she'd ever experienced on a project.

Sewing the final garments together had always been Patricia's least favourite part of the whole knitting process. She loved dreaming up the ideas, choosing colours and sourcing the perfect yarn... she loved the knitting itself too, of course... but sewing up – not so much. It had something to do with her secret hate of actually handing a finished garment over. She knew it was ridiculous, but it was always a huge wrench for her - she became attached to every piece she worked on. Maybe that's why designing this collection for such a massive audience was freaking her out more than she'd expected.

At least her original sketches for the collection had survived the deluge. She'd taped them to the walls, and other than a few splatters here and there that had slightly warped a few of the pages, the drawings themselves had survived.

Patricia stared at them, crossing her arms and trying to ignore the sense of unease that crept into her chest. This was the first time she'd ever considered working with a label to mass-produce her designs, and she still wasn't completely sure how she felt about it. In the end, the team at Butter had been so enthusiastic about working with her, telling her that they simply wouldn't take "no" for an answer. And so, she'd said yes!

Of course, the other members of *Knit One Pour One* had been over the moon for her when she'd shared the news with them. They'd erupted in a wave of cheering, congratulations and chatter, and she'd spent the entire evening being told what a wonderful opportunity it was for her. According to everyone there, it was about time she got the recognition she deserved.

Patricia wasn't so sure. She'd been really touched by their excitement of course, and there was definitely something special about elevating a craft and giving it prominence on the national stage… but she had to admit that she'd found the process pretty daunting right from the moment Butter had expressed their interest in her work. It was usually such a private experience, and now there was an entire team of people waiting to see what she came up with. It was more than enough to scare her rigid!

That was the reality of her recent bad mood. Yes, meeting Harry had certainly unsettled her - but this had been going on a lot longer than that. What if no one liked the designs she came up with? What then?

She'd had tons of conversations with Butter's creative team – but none of them had really helped. They just kept telling her that they loved her aesthetic and that they didn't want her to feel pushed in any particular direction. It should have been the perfect way to work.

She was sure it was as rare as hen's teeth to find a label to work with who just wanted her to do her own thing.

The problem was – with all that freedom, she hadn't been able to stop herself from questioning if "her own thing" would end up being good enough.

Looking at her sketches now - all set out in front of her on the wall - it felt like her worst nightmare had come true. It wasn't that they weren't good enough - the problem was that they simply weren't *her*.

Patricia's style had always been pretty grungy – she loved everything oversized, with gorgeous little vintage touches thrown in. The key thing for her was comfort. She loved chunky and soft… a little bit saggy, baggy and almost a pre-loved look. In her book, that was knitwear you could fall in love with.

This collection she'd been working on was the polar opposite of that. These designs were sharp and lean, tailored with geometric designs at the collar and neckline. They were perfect for expensive, sensitive yarns and were aimed at customers who loved high fashion and "dressing up". They definitely weren't for people like her. Or people like Harry.

'Oh, for goodness's sake!' sighed Patricia. Here she was desperately trying to get her head back into work-mode despite everything - and there he was again - popping up in her head to distract her.

Or… maybe it wasn't a distraction… maybe her subconscious was trying to tell her something. Harry might not be the target market for the collection she'd been working on... but he could certainly rock a nicely knitted jumper. The one he'd been wearing when he'd rescued her from falling into the river had almost made her swoon as much as the man himself!

A simple man's jumper... oversized... beautiful yarn... stunningly knitted.

Suddenly the problem was so obvious, it was like being hit with it between the eyes. The reason she hadn't been able to get on with her work and save her collection after the flood was staring at her... she simply didn't like her designs. They weren't her style at all. They were flashy and showy and had no soul.

That was the problem with trying to prove herself to a bunch of people she was desperate to impress... she'd stopped trusting her own judgement. They'd given her absolute control and she'd promptly double-guessed everything she'd ever designed and every creative impulse she'd ever had.

'Well... shit,' she breathed, running her hand over the nearest piece of knitted jacket. She'd washed them to get rid of the plaster dust and manky water and had then pinned them all out while they dried so that they hadn't lost their shape. She felt no emotional attachment to any of it which wasn't like her at all.

Well, one thing was for sure – she'd need to get a second opinion before she went any further. It looked like she couldn't trust her own instincts when it came to this project. The problem now was, who should she ask?

There was no way she was going to speak to her contact at Butter again – that would be totally unprofessional – especially after she'd already asked them for a delay on the meeting because of the leak. They'd been incredibly kind and understanding. She didn't want them finding out that instead of working with a professional creative, they'd actually managed to land themselves a hot mess who just happened to own a whole bunch of knitting needles.

The obvious choice would be to ask the *Knit One Pour One* crew for their input - but there was no way she could do that. Sure, she'd get plenty of feedback – but it was also the fastest way to ensure the whole story would be all over Bamton Ford, Upper Bamton – and perhaps even as far as Little Bamton and Seabury by the following morning. It didn't matter that the gossip would probably be good-natured, Patricia was having a hard enough time on this project without having to navigate continuous questions from the locals for months to come!

But... maybe there was someone else she could ask. Someone who ticked all the boxes. Harry.

He might not be an obvious choice, but the man clearly knew a good jumper when he saw one. He wasn't local. Patricia wasn't sure where he was from, but she knew everyone in Bamton Ford and Upper Bamton. Sure, he was James's dad, but James had so much on his plate at the moment that there was no way the pair of them would be likely to spend any time gossiping about knitting patterns!

Add to that the fact that Harry didn't have anything invested in the project, he wasn't a super-keen knitting fan… and he currently spent a decent amount of time just outside her cottage. He was basically perfect.

Right. Decision made. She'd ask Harry. Now all she needed to do was drum up the courage to actually approach him.

CHAPTER 7

The decision to ask Harry for his input had galvanized Patricia into action for the first time in what felt like weeks. She'd spent the rest of the afternoon and evening… and, if she was being honest, most of the night too… tacking the various pieces together. She didn't want to do a proper, finished job in case she needed to pull them all apart to help her get the patterns down on paper.

After she'd finished stitching the fifth one, her fingers were throbbing and she resorted to using pins wherever she could get away with it. The main thing was that she needed items that would hold together for long enough for Harry to get a proper feel for them, rather than just showing him the sketches. That's if she managed to summon the courage to actually ask him for his opinion.

When she had finally fallen into bed at something

silly o'clock in the morning, her fingers ached, her neck was sore and her eyelids were begging to close. It was fair to say that she was absolutely exhausted, but as she yawned her way into sleep, it didn't take long for Patricia's predictions from earlier in the day had come true.

No matter how close an eye she'd kept on all things Harry through the window during her slightly-more-regular-than-usual coffee breaks, sadly there hadn't been a re-run of the wet tee-shirt performance. When he'd come back from his lunch break, Patricia had been rather gutted that Harry had discovered his waterproofs.

Still, it seemed that her subconscious mind had stored the image away to taunt her with all night. Yet again she'd been faced with the bike ride from hell, heading straight for the whirling vortex of water. This time, though, Harry hadn't just saved her from a dunking. He'd also featured as a Mr Darcy-esque character, wandering around in her dreamscape in a wet tee shirt, dripping in the most distracting way.

The day had started out with yet more heavy rain. She glared at the heavy drops as she waited for the kettle to boil. After all her hard work, Patricia had to admit the idea of Harry not turning up to work on the Ferry because of the weather was not giving her the most zen-like of vibes. In fact, the idea had been plaguing her ever since she'd woken up and forced her knackered limbs into the shower.

In the grand scheme of things, another day before

she had the chance to ask him for his opinion wouldn't be that big a deal. The thing was – after being stuck for so long – she suddenly had some momentum and she didn't want to lose it again. Now that she'd started down this path, she just wanted to hear his thoughts and then figure out what she was going to do next.

As far as she could tell, she had three options open to her – finish the current designs, put together a whole new collection in a matter of days, or cancel the whole thing entirely. Right now, all three of them made her feel slightly queasy.

As Patricia poured herself another cup of coffee in the vague hope that it might wake her up a bit, she heard a roar start up outside on the riverbank. Heading straight for the window, she spotted Harry and breathed a sigh of relief.

The rain seemed to have stopped briefly – which should have made it the perfect moment to dash out and make her request. Sadly though, Harry had clearly decided to make the most of the momentary lull by firing up a power sander. Blimey, it was a noisy beast – and by the look of things, it was going to kick up an awful lot of dust too.

It didn't take long for her to come to the conclusion that the dust wasn't actually going to make much of a mess… on the ground at least. The wind was whipping it straight at Harry and it was busy glueing itself all over him like a very unexciting layer of glitter.

Patricia started to giggle as she watched him pause

for a moment to wipe two little peep-holes in the thick layer of grime that had already coated his safety goggles. Blimey – poor bloke, having to work out there in these conditions!

She glanced up at the sky, wondering how long it'd be before the rain kicked off again. By the looks of things, it was already gearing back up for another deluge.

Right then – it was now or never.

Patricia plonked her half-drunk cup of coffee down onto the kitchen table and, heading over to the door, she slipped her wellies. Heading outside, she wandered across the sodden, grassy bank to where Harry was still valiantly wielding the sander. The whole front of him had turned the same off-white as the boat's hull – thick with a layer of glued-on dust.

Coming to a standstill, she waited quietly for a moment, eyeing Harry as he focused on the job in front of him. The last thing she wanted to do was make him jump by appearing out of nowhere, but equally the sander was so loud she wasn't sure how to get his attention without startling him.

After a couple of minutes of fidgety indecision on her part, Harry clearly sensed that he was being watched. He flicked the switch on the sander and turned towards her, pushing his goggles up onto his forehead.

Patricia had to bite her lip – the effect was like some kind of bizarre, inverted panda eyes. The skin under the goggles was the only part of Harry's face that wasn't coated in a thick layer of the pale dust. His's eyes stared back at her from the middle of all the mess, and she caught her breath. She hadn't noticed how lovely they were. Hazel with bright flecks of green, as though they were scattered with emeralds.

Harry smiled at her, and Patricia started to giggle. She couldn't help it – his teeth were covered in dust too. What a mess!

'What?!' said Harry, looking confused.

'Sorry,' chuckled Patricia. 'You've got a bit of…' she pointed at her own mouth vaguely and then shrugged. 'A bit of dust?'

Harry smirked. 'A bit of an understatement, that,' he said, running his hands through his hair and ending up with badger stripes. 'Anyway, what's up?'

'Erm – I wanted to speak with you… if you've got a moment?'

Harry gave her a nod and stashed the sander under the upturned boat, clearly in an attempt to keep it safe if it started to rain again.

'Fire away,' he said, turning back to her.

'Maybe inside?' said Patricia, glancing up at the sky.

'Oh. Okay, fine,' he said.

Patricia couldn't help but notice that he didn't seem particularly enthusiastic about it. Well… that wasn't exactly the start she'd been hoping for, but she couldn't back out now could she? She really needed his help!

The pair of them trudged back up towards the

house, with Harry trailing a little way behind Patricia the whole way. She led the way around to the front door, and Harry followed her into the hallway, stopping just past the welcome mat. It felt a bit like she was leading a stubborn donkey. Patricia turned to smile at him, hoping to lighten the mood before she actually had to ask him for the favour.

'You okay?' she said, raising an eyebrow. It was clear from his body language that Harry thought he was in for some kind of telling off. She'd just opened her mouth to reassure him when he beat her to it and started to apologise.

'If it's the noise, I'm really sorry - but I've got to get this work done somehow. This bloody weather... I mean, this blooming weather...' he corrected himself. 'Sorry,' he said again. 'It's ruining my sandpaper. I had to get on with it this morning as soon as the rain stopped – but I promise I'll be finished as quickly as I can. There isn't much more to do.'

He paused and scuffed his foot on the flagstones.

'Actually, that's a lie,' he added. 'The ferry's in a pretty poor state, but I should be able to finish off the sanding this morning. Maybe. If I get a wiggle on.'

Patricia listened to his whole apology in silent amusement. When he'd finished, she had to take a couple of seconds to compose herself and make sure that she wasn't about to giggle in his face.

'It's not the noise,' she said at last, her lips twitching with the effort.

Harry visibly relaxed. The tiny movement made Patricia glance down at the grubby puddle of dusty rainwater that was forming under his feet as he stood there, gently dripping. Clearly, bringing Harry into her hallway was as bad as bringing her bicycle indoors.

Harry followed her gaze and frowned. 'Oops,' he said. 'Hmm… maybe I'd better…' he stripped off his wet raincoat and hung it on the newel post. Then he pulled his sweater over his head and draped it over the top.

'Good idea,' croaked Patricia. Hell, standing quite so close to the man while he disrobed was having quite an effect on her. 'Though maybe the jumper should go over the bannisters – you don't want it to stretch.'

'Right you are,' grunted Harry, 'you're the expert.'

Patricia reached over and shifted the sweater so that it was draped carefully over the smooth, sweeping wood of the bannisters. It wasn't too wet – just damp around the cuff and the neck where the rain had started to seep under Harry's coat. It was a different jumper to the one he'd been wearing that first day she'd met him – but just like the other one, it was hand-knitted and really beautifully made. The design was clever but not overly intricate. She noticed that the cuffs were starting to fray a bit – but that was only to be expected. She'd noticed that Harry liked to roll his sleeves up while he was working, and that was bound to take its toll. Maybe she could offer to repair it in exchange for his help.

'There,' she said, stroking the soft wool one last time, making sure it was secure. The woolly was heavy enough that it didn't slide down the bannister. It wasn't the perfect solution – but at least this way it wouldn't end up with a great big stretched-out bulge from the top of the newel post!

'Erm... thanks?' said Harry.

Patricia turned back to him and smiled. His tee shirt was only a little bit damp where around his shoulders and the top of his back.

What a shame!

Patria gave herself a little shake. She wanted Harry's opinion on something important... she hadn't brought him inside to ogle the poor man!

'Right,' she said. Now that she had him here, she couldn't help wondering how she was meant to actually ask for his help.

They seem to have got stuck in the narrow hallway, and now that Harry was standing there in just his tee shirt with his strong arms on show, her brain seem to have become muddled.

Patricia could feel the warmth coming from his skin, and that *really* wasn't helping her think straight... but she'd better get on and do something quickly, otherwise the poor guy was going to start to steam.

'Let's go through to the kitchen,' she said, her voice ever so slightly hoarse.

Harry nodded and gave a little shrug but didn't budge. That's when Patricia realised that, of course, he'd never been inside the house before. He didn't have a clue as to the layout.

'Erm… follow me,' she said, feeling stupid.

Pushing open the kitchen door, Patricia made a beeline for the kettle and flicked it. She needed more coffee to get her through this! She turned back to Harry, only to find him paused just inside the door, looking around the room in wonder.

Looking at it through someone else's eyes, she realised that her kitchen probably made her look more than a little bit eccentric… but she wasn't about to start apologising for surrounding herself with things that made her happy.

It was a lovely room - old-fashioned, with low beams. Right in the middle sat a large, scrubbed pine table. She'd filled one wall with sketches for pattern ideas and test squares of knitting. Another one held her collection of pictures and paintings of people spinning wool. There were several baskets dotted around the room, piled high with odd balls of yarn – leftovers from various projects – and, of course, the ever-present jugs filled with knitting needles sat on almost every surface.

She glanced at Harry, wondering if he was about to make a dash for it, but he was busy examining one of her favourite sketches. She was surprised by how good it felt to see someone looking at her work with such obvious appreciation. She gave a tiny little wriggle of happiness and then froze as Harry turned to her.

'Am I right in thinking that... I'm not in trouble?' he said carefully.

Patricia grinned at the big guy in front of her who suddenly looked more like a naughty schoolboy.

'Nope – you're not in trouble,' she laughed.

'So what...?'

'Well, Harry... I was wondering if you might be up for doing me a favour...?'

CHAPTER 8

'But... I don't know anything about knitting!' said Harry, looking completely bemused. He was clearly struggling to understand her request.

'Well,' said Patricia, calmly turning back to the kettle and pouring a cup of coffee for them both without even asking if he wanted one, 'you do have a collection of very nice jumpers.'

In her head, that explained everything. Unfortunately, when she turned back to face Harry, the look he was giving her told her that it didn't explain anything – and that she was verging on *insane knitting lady* territory again.

'My grandmother knitted those jumpers, not me,' said Harry with a little laugh. 'I've had them for years... she actually knitted them for my dad originally and then I pilfered them. I've had them for years... I wear them all the time – they just seem to keep on going!'

'She must have been really quite something with those knitting needles!' said Patricia, plonking two fresh cups of coffee onto the table and indicating for Harry to sit down.

'Erm – do you mind if I wash up at the sink first?' said Harry, raising his dust-encrusted hands.

'Sorry!' said Patricia quickly, 'of course.'

Harry nodded his thanks, strode to the sink, turned on her cold tap and grabbed the gritty cake of yellow soap that had been sitting on her windowsill for years. It was one of those that never seemed to come to an end. She'd been meaning to buy something a bit more genteel for ages, but never seemed to get around to it. It didn't seem to bother Harry though, as he proceeded to lather up his hands, then his arms all the way up to the elbows.

Patricia swallowed a mouthful of coffee, unable to tear her eyes away from the way the muscles in his back moved under his fine tee shirt as he worked. Boy, she'd been on her own for *far* too long if watching a man washing his hands could get her all hot and bothered! She watched, completely spellbound, as Harry dipped his head and started to sluice the crusted dust away from his face. She just about managed to unfreeze from her trance when he turned to her, eyes scrunched closed, his chin dripping.

'Erm... got a towel? That soap is vicious!'

'Of course!' she said, scooting straight out of her chair. She grabbed the fluffy hand towel from its hook and thrust it into his blindly-outstretched hands.

'Ta!' he said, mopping his face dry and blinking fast, clearly trying to clear soap suds from his eyes. At least he'd managed to wash away the inverted panda dust mask he'd been rocking.

'You okay?' said Patricia.

'Much better – thanks!' laughed Harry. He draped the towel over the bar at the front of the aga, then made his way back to the table and sat down opposite her. 'Now... what were we talking about?'

'Your grandma's knitting,' said Patricia, forcing herself to stop staring at his lovely face and focus on blowing the steam from her coffee for a moment instead.

'Right... right... well, yeah – she was *always* knitting. It was a bit of a running joke in our family. We used to have to turn the TV up because of her clicking knitting needles!'

'Did she live with you?' asked Patricia, keen to get to know a bit more about him.

Harry nodded. 'Came to live with us after my grandpa passed away. She was a lovely old woman... gentle and sweet and wise. She could keep a secret too and was always on our side – me and my brother. Plus, you were guaranteed a new jumper every Christmas and birthday!'

'Lucky you!' said Patricia.

'Not really something a teenaged lad knows how to appreciate! But now I can see how much love and effort went into every single stitch. You know, I haven't thought about it for years, but I kind of miss the constant clacking.'

'I don't suppose you know what happened to her patterns?' Patricia was unable to stop herself from asking. After losing so many of her own, she was keen to start building her collection back up as soon as possible.

'She never seemed to work from a pattern – not that I remember anyway. Though, she always had a scrap of card torn from an old greetings card next to her, and this funny, stubby little pencil. She'd use them to jot down numbers and symbols as she went along… wow, there's another thing I haven't thought about in forever!' he said with a soft smile.

Patricia smiled back and nodded. 'Keeping track of her lines and stitches.'

'I guess so,' he said. 'It must have worked – her jumpers always seemed to turn out perfectly.' He paused and took a sip of his coffee. 'Now then – you mentioned that you needed my help with something knitting-related?'

Patricia nodded slowly. She felt kind of foolish now it came down to it. Harry seemed to be lovely, but was he *really* the right person to ask for advice on something like this? Well, she couldn't exactly change her mind now that she'd dragged him in here, could she?

'I wanted to ask your advice on something. Well… your opinion, really.'

'Oh?' he said, cocking his head adorably and looking intrigued.

'I've been working on this knitwear line for a company… a series of designs… on and off now for a few months.'

She paused and sucked in a deep breath. It had definitely been more off than on for quite a while now. Something she'd realised as she'd been stitching the garments together the night before was that her flooded studio had actually just been a damn good excuse to stop work. An excuse - but not the real reason.

'I'm not sure how I can help with that,' laughed Harry. 'I keep telling you – I can't knit!'

'Well, I need an outside eye on them before I finish them off and present them to the company I'm working with. That's all I'm asking - for you to have a look at them and tell me what you think.'

'Surely you'd be better asking that knitting group you and James go to?'

Patricia sighed and shook her head. 'They're all a bit too… keen. I love them all to bits, but they're so excited about this project that I think they'd tell me they loved anything I showed them. Plus – I could do with it not being all over the village.'

Harry let out a deep, belly laugh at that. 'Small village gossip vines, eh?'

'Something like that,' she said, smiling at him. 'So – will you do it?'

'You want me to be honest?'

Patricia nodded. 'Definitely.'

Somehow, she had a feeling that Harry was the kind of guy who'd be incapable of giving you anything other than his honest opinion. She might know very little about him, but from what she'd seen so far, he seemed to be a straight arrow - a no-nonsense kind of bloke. Just the kind she liked. Just the kind that didn't seem to come along very often.

'Okay,' said Harry. 'If you think it'll help, I'll do it.'

'Great! Thank you so much.' said Patricia, getting to her feet.

'What – you want to do it now?' said Harry, staring at her in surprise.

'Now's the perfect time,' she said, pointing at the window.

Harry looked over and sighed. It was piddling with rain again.

'It won't take long,' she said. 'I've got everything laid out upstairs.'

'Okay then,' said Harry, getting to his feet and looking vaguely amused at the strange direction his day had taken.

Patricia led the way out of the kitchen and up the stairs with her heart thudding in her chest. She kept trying to convince herself that it was because she was nervous about what Harry was going to say about her work. In reality, it was a physical response to the simple act of leading Harry upstairs. There hadn't been a man up here in years, let alone a man she'd spent the last several nights having increasingly x-rated night-time dream-romps with!

'What's that noise?' asked Harry as he reached the landing.

'Dehumidifiers,' mumbled Patricia, willing herself to calm down. 'I was going to say – excuse the mess. I had a water leak in my studio. I'm still trying to get everything dried out.'

'Nightmare!' said Harry sympathetically.

'You could say that,' she sighed. 'Anyway, come on in.'

The pieces were already laid out across the two trestle tables. Patricia had wanted to be ready. She knew that she might have to grab Harry on of his rare coffee breaks, and she hadn't wanted to waste any time if the opportunity arose.

She quickly flicked the dehumidifiers off to give them a bit of peace and quiet and pointed Harry in the direction of the tables.

As Harry moved forwards and stared down at her knitting, Patricia watched his face closely. She couldn't help but notice that he looked a bit nonplussed by the whole thing.

'Oh,' he said, staring from one piece to the next.

Patricia raised her eyebrows, resisting the temptation to jump straight in and start asking questions.

What did that mean though?

Did he like them?

Didn't he like them?

Harry wandered backwards and forwards a couple of times, unconsciously fiddling with the stubble on his chin. Patricia managed to keep shtum for all of ten seconds before she couldn't wait any longer.

'What do you think?' She promptly cringed. She didn't want to sound like a six-year-old asking for praise... but she desperately needed some feedback here.

'I'm... I'm not sure!' said Harry. 'I mean, I guess I thought they'd be on a mannequin... or a dummy... something like you'd see in a shop window.' He shrugged and looked along the line again.

Patricia followed his eyes. All those hours of work laid out before him.

'They kind of look a bit lifeless laid out flat, don't you think? I'm not sure I can tell you what I think without seeing them on a body... maybe I just don't have the right sort of imagination!'

'No, you're right,' said Patricia. 'Clothes are meant to be worn. They're meant to move.'

'Exactly,' said Harry, turning to her and giving another little shrug. 'Sorry. I told you I'd be useless at this.'

'Not useless,' said Patricia quickly. 'Already really helpful!'

She took a step forwards and stroked the collar of one of the pieces. It had been a total bitch to get right.

'Maybe I can model them for you?' she said, then promptly clamped her mouth shut. Where had *that* come from?! The words had just appeared on her tongue out of nowhere. She was *such* an idiot.

'Yeah – great,' said Harry. 'That might help. I'd definitely get a better idea.'

Awkward!

Patricia was suddenly acutely aware that she hadn't bothered to put her bra back on after her morning shower. She could see it now, in her mind's eye, hooked over the towel rail in the bathroom. To model everything for Harry, she'd have to take her sweater off. Sure, she was wearing a tee-shirt underneath… but it'd still be pretty obvious. She couldn't back out now, though.

She could always nip out and slip her bra back on… but… maybe she was overthinking this. Then again, maybe not. The usually airy space felt strangely small and cramped with the two large dehumidifiers and an extra person in it. An extra *man*. Harry was the first man ever to grace her studio… and she was feeling decidedly wrong-footed. The last thing she needed was her dingly danglies… *dingly dangly-ing* all over the place,

Grow up!

Patricia could feel the blush creeping onto her face, but as she glanced at Harry he seemed to be totally oblivious to her discomfort. He was staring at her work again.

She needed to get on with this before the rain stopped and Harry needed to get back to work on the boat. Patricia glanced around the studio. There was quite literally nowhere private to change. She could always try clambering under the table – but that would simply be ridiculous. The only other option was to attempt to change behind the curtains – but quite frankly, she was more likely to be spotted by someone idiot enough to be pottering around outside.

'Okay, let's do this…' she said, 'but would you mind turning around while I change?'

Harry looked amused rather than embarrassed. Well, at least that made one of them!

'Sure thing,' he said. 'I can go and stand outside if you'd prefer?'

Just the fact that he offered made Patricia relax a tiny bit. She shook her head. 'There are loads of them to get through… that could get silly!' she smiled at him. 'I won't take a second.'

Harry just nodded and turned around to face the door. Patricia hastily stripped off her own jumper – and was instantly grateful that he wasn't looking, as her white tee-shirt rode right up. Phew, that would have given him a right eyeful!

She yanked it back into place and slipped into the first item from the trestle table. Somehow she just about managed to resist the temptation to do something stupid like whistling a fanfare to get Harry to turn around.

'Ready,' she said, cursing the slight shake in her voice.

Harry turned slowly back to face her.

CHAPTER 9

Patricia had managed to get a dozen designs ready in time to show Harry. With every change of clothes so far, he'd dutifully turned his back - he might have huffed and puffed a bit about it, but in a silly, playful way that put Patricia at her ease. Very quickly, the ridiculousness of the situation had become a bit of a running joke between the pair of them, and there was a lot more laughter going on than Patricia had been expecting.

So far, Harry had resisted saying anything about her work – claiming that he wanted to get a feel for the whole collection before giving her any feedback.

'Fine,' sighed Patricia, having begged for a comment - any comment - on item number four. 'Go on then…'

'Turn around?' asked Harry, starting to giggle.

Patricia snorted. 'Turn around!'

She didn't know why the pair of them were finding everything so funny by this point – maybe because it had gone from the sublime to the ridiculous. Harry promptly executed a comedy triple-pirouette before settling to face in the opposite direction.

It took them both several minutes to get over their giggles before Patricia was ready to pull on the next jumper.

'Okay, ready.'

Harry turned to face her and grinned as she struck a pose, then his expression turned solemn as he got back to the job at hand.

Patricia had to bite her lip. Every single time they got to this bit, she struggled to hold back the litany of excuses she wanted to make about her work. She only just managed to hold them back because she didn't want to colour his thoughts in any way.

One thing was certain though, she was very glad Harry had agreed to do this for her. It had confirmed beyond all doubt that she wasn't ready to show the collection to Butter just yet – not when she squirmed with embarrassment with every single piece she put on. By this point in proceedings, she knew that her unease had nothing to do with changing – braless - within such close proximity to Harry, and everything to do with the knitwear itself.

Harry looked the tunic she was now wearing up and down and then, with a gesture, got her to slowly turn on the spot so that he could take a look at the back.

Patricia sighed. Something was solidifying in her heart…

'Next,' said Harry.

Patricia grabbed the hem of the tunic and yanked it off without asking Harry to turn around. After all, she was wearing a tee shirt and frankly, the amount of giggling was just getting silly now. Besides – Harry seemed to be so focused on taking in every detail of her work that she didn't think he'd even notice her bra-less state by this point.

'Right, so… not bothering with the whole "turn around" thing anymore?' asked Harry lightly.

Patricia just shrugged and grabbed a striped blazer with a ludicrously intricate pattern worked into the side panels. She'd been so relieved that this jacket hadn't been damaged by the burst pipe because – if she was being honest – she couldn't face sitting down to knit the blasted thing again. Unfortunately, the pattern had bitten the dust, and she was dreading trying to recreate the whole thing on paper again… it had been hard enough to capture the first time around!

'There!' she said, doing up the woven tie-belt and putting her hands on her hips.

Harry stared at the blazer with a raised eyebrow.

It was that eyebrow that did it. Just like before, excuses and apologies rose in Patricia's throat… but this time she completely failed to hold them in.

'It's not quite finished... I know the front panels still need a bit of work. When it's stitched up properly rather than pinned, it should hold its shape better...'

Harry just shrugged and moved around her to look at it from different angles.

'I'm not sure what I was thinking with that line of pattern across the back, I...' she let her excuse trail away.

There wasn't any point in doing this anymore, was there? It no longer really mattered what Harry was going to say when they got to the end of the samples - she was boring herself. This work was dull and lifeless. If she had to explain what she'd been thinking with design, then the design wasn't working.

She dropped her pose and shook her hands out at her sides. Suddenly, everything was crystal clear. Her instincts yesterday had been spot on. The reason she'd been dragging her heels and putting off doing the work to finish this collection was that she didn't really like the pieces... any of them.

Patricia rubbed her face roughly as the reality of the situation started to sink in. She'd wasted so much time, and the delivery deadline was just around the corner. She had days and hours left rather than weeks and months.

'I knew this was a bad idea,' she whispered.

'Oh god, I'm sorry,' said Harry. 'I did warn you that I was probably the last person who should be helping you with this!'

'No!' said Patricia, her head snapping up to stare at Harry in horror. 'No – sorry – I didn't mean you! Definitely not you… it's me that's the problem.' She turned and rested her hand on one of the discarded jumpers. 'I don't know what I was thinking with these,' she sighed. 'They're not really my style at all… it's not what I do.'

She paused and turned to look at Harry, but he just stared quietly back at her, waiting for her to continue.

'I… I just desperately wanted to impress this company. I mean – they wanted to work with me – which is a huge deal. So… I went and tried to do something new and different… when I should have just been…'

'You?' said Harry.

'Me,' Patricia nodded.

Harry smiled. 'I can see what you were going for with these, though,' he said, coming to stand beside her. They both peered at the dozens of hours of wasted work laid out in front of them. 'I mean, they're amazing. Beautiful work. But… maybe they're all just a bit busy – that's all.'

Patricia let out a sigh. Harry was right.

'But then – what do I know? You're not designing them for someone like me. I just love something simple - and not these fine, lightweight jobbies either… I'd put a hole in them in a second. I like my woollies cosy, warm and hard-wearing. But like I said… that's just me. I'm not exactly up there at the height of fashion, am I?!'

Patricia turned and looked him up and down. Grubby jeans, damp tee-shirt and tousled hair. When she reached his kind and stupidly handsome face, she broke into a smile. She couldn't help but think how good he'd looked in his grandmother's jumpers. They were simple, beautifully made and suited his body shape perfectly.

Suddenly, Patricia felt the tingling of a new idea blossoming somewhere deep inside her. Inspiration prickled its way along her spine. Maybe she'd been taking these designs in the wrong direction all along. Perhaps if she used the simple lines of a man's over-sized sweater as her starting point... maybe she'd get somewhere that felt a little bit more... her? It would definitely be several steps closer to the way she liked her knitwear...

'You okay?' said Harry. He was eyeing her with a mixture of amusement and concern.

Patricia nodded slowly, her brain flooded with half-formed ideas and images – it was that glorious rush that she'd not experienced since she'd been given this opportunity.

'Wait here one minute,' she gasped. 'I just want to try something.'

Doing her best to ignore the look of pure confusion on Harry's face, Patricia dashed from the room and hurried down the stairs. Reaching the flagstones of the hallway, she grabbed Harry's jumper from its spot on the bannisters. It was still wet, but that didn't really matter.

She quickly unravelled herself from the half-finished, complicated blazer and threw it unceremoniously over the newel post before slipping Harry's jumper over her head.

It was huge – almost coming down to her knees. She turned to face the hall mirror for a second and gave herself a little nod. This was even better than she'd hoped. She undid her jeans and wiggled them down to her feet. There. The perfect sweater dress!

Why hadn't she considered one as part of her collection before? It was right up her street, and probably the sort of thing the guys at Butter were expecting from her anyway… instead of the weird, geometric nonsense she'd been struggling to bring to life for so many months.

Patricia stepped out of her jeans fully so that Harry would be able to see the full effect for himself when she went back upstairs. It was clear that he was a *show don't tell* kind of guy.

As an after-thought, she yanked the elastic out of her long hair and dragged her fingers through it before turning back to the mirror to check the full effect. Hmm – one more thing… she stooped and yanked her socks off. There, that was better. Now the jumper showed off a pair of nice, toned legs… all that cycling had to have some benefits!

Giving herself a quick smile, she turned and scampered back up the stairs, bursting in on Harry... who froze in place, his eyes widening.

Patricia didn't bother to strike a pose this time. There simply wasn't any need... it was obvious that Harry was speechless, and she just stood there grinning at him.

He opened his mouth to say something, but then closed it again.

'Come on,' she laughed, 'what do you think?'

'Erm... wow?!' he said with a slow grin as he looked her up and down.

Patricia's smile widened. With Harry's help, she'd cracked it. After all this time working on ideas and samples, heading down increasingly complex routes, she should have just followed her instincts and kept things simple all along.

Now she knew what she had to do. She'd start again. Each design would be based on Harry's grandmother's jumpers – with her own unique twists and turns added along the way.

A shiver of delight ran down her spine. *This* was what it was meant to feel like... not the huge lump of dread she'd been carrying around with her for so long.

Without giving it a second thought, Patricia stepped forward and kissed Harry on his bristly cheek.

'Thank you,' she whispered, pulling back and meeting his beautiful eyes.

Harry just stared straight back at her, and time seemed to pause for a long moment. Patricia could feel every beat of her heart. Her skin prickled as she gazed back at him, her breathing loud in her ears. See – this was what came from asking a gorgeous man for his opinion and then stealing his jumper.

The exact same moment as Patricia reached for Harry, his own arms wound around her waist, drawing her in.

Suddenly all Patricia's worries melted away. Nothing mattered – not the deadlines, the rain hammering down outside, or the fact that she wasn't wearing a bra… or trousers for that matter!

Harry's soft lips found hers and Patricia sighed as she melted into the kiss. Well… this certainly beat staring at him out of a window!

'You're all wet!' said Harry, pulling back, his hands patting the damp patches on her improvised sweater dress.

Patricia let out a snort of surprised laughter. 'Did you seriously just say that?'

Harry's eyes widened in momentary horror and then he started to chuckle. 'I did… I did just say that!' he howled, his whole body shaking with laughter now.

'You're right though,' said Patricia, taking a tiny step back. Some kind of naughty spirit seemed to be in the process of body-snatching her. She didn't really know this man – she had no idea where he lived or what he did… or even what his surname was – but right now, none of that mattered. The wave of inspiration and exhilaration coursing through her body meant that, for once, she knew exactly what she wanted.

Slowly, reaching for the hem of the jumper and holding his gaze until the last possible moment, she drew it up over her head.

CHAPTER 10

Patricia placed her loaded needles down on the little table next to her armchair, making sure that her work-in-progress wasn't about to slip onto the floor before getting to her feet. She rotated her tired wrists and then flexed her fingers, trying to get the feeling back in them. She'd never knitted so intensely before... and she was starting to feel the effects. Not that she minded one little bit... every single ache, pain and twinge was more than worth it.

The past few days had disappeared in a blur of activity. Patricia had decided to start her collection right from square one. With just a matter of days left to get it all done, she'd been flat-out - researching, sketching, choosing yarns and making emergency orders for fresh supplies.

Then, of course, there was knitting, knitting and

more knitting. She was working into the wee small hours of the morning – only to fall into bed when she couldn't keep her eyes open a moment longer. Five minutes later (or at least, that's what it felt like to her) she'd be getting dressed, loading herself with yet more coffee and starting work all over again. The big difference was – now that she was working on something she believed in - she was enjoying every aching, agonising, knackering second of it!

Patricia turned on the spot, rolling her shoulders and trying to ease out the knots as she stared at the kitchen walls. She'd pinned up her new sketches with their corresponding patterns alongside them, and had been constantly tweaking and revising them as she went along. She'd learned her lesson this time though, and made sure that she snapped a new photograph on her mobile every time they were altered.

Six beautiful men's jumpers hung from the picture rail on the back wall. She'd managed to convince Harry to loan her every single piece he still owned that had been knitted by his grandmother. Harry had been more than happy to oblige – on the condition that in return, Patricia would not only mend the fraying hems and any little holes she could find, but also agree to knit him two brand new jumpers of her own design. After she'd finished her current project, of course.

Patricia was more than happy with his terms. It was just the sort of trade-off that made sense to her yarn-obsessed brain. As she'd carefully arranged the six borrowed pullovers on their padded hangers, she felt like she was the one getting the best side of the deal!

As expected, Harry's jumpers had been the inspiration for the fifteen new designs Patricia was now busy slaving away over. And – at long last - she was getting somewhere. Perhaps even more importantly, she was excited about this new work, and she couldn't wait to present them to the team at Butter in a few days' time.

She was actually looking forward to her meeting in London now, whereas before she'd been dreading it. She hadn't worked this hard in such a long time – perhaps ever. But now that she knew exactly what she wanted to achieve with this collection, it suddenly felt worthwhile putting in all the hours it would take to get there. Sleep be damned – this was exactly what caffeine had been invented for! On that note...

Patricia wandered over to the counter to flick the kettle on, still trying to loosen up the muscles in her back and neck as she went. This was probably the fifth or sixth drink she'd made for herself today. She'd only managed a sip or two of each one before abandoning them in a daze. She kept finding the mugs dotted around the house hours later - still full to the brim with cold coffee, complete with a gross layer of skin.

Patricia took all this as a good sign, though. This level of distraction meant that she was totally engrossed in what she was doing – to the detriment of everything else. The project was now taking up every waking moment - and most of the moments she should have been asleep too.

Well... when she said *every* waking moment... she did have to admit that she still treated herself to the occasional trip to the window... just to *check* on Harry. But that was fine, wasn't it? He *was* her muse, after all!

Harry seemed to understand just how much she had on her plate and how little time she had left to get everything done. After dropping off the jumpers, he'd stayed well out of her way. It wasn't as though they were avoiding each other or anything... or, at least, she hoped they weren't.

The other day had been... incredible. Fired by the explosion of inspiration and her mad, bubbling desire for Harry that had been building from the moment he'd saved her from a plunge into the river, Patricia had lost all her inhibitions. All she could say for Harry was that, after a brief moment of pure surprise, he hadn't seemed to mind in the slightest.

Now, as she worked, Patricia had to keep telling herself that she wasn't embarrassed by how she'd behaved. Okay, so maybe she was... just a tiny bit... but there was nothing she could do about all that right now, was there?

They both had a deadline looming – her with getting the collection finished and ready to present, and him with getting the ferry back in the water in time for the Bamton Abbey Open Day. So - he'd stayed out of her way, and she'd stayed out of his. It didn't mean anything bad. Not at all. It just meant that they were both ridiculously busy.

Patricia sighed. She hadn't even ventured outside to take him a hot drink – the weather was just too grim, and she didn't want to have to go through the paralarva of having to make sure she was completely clean and dry before getting back to work. She just couldn't risk any damage to her work this close to the deadline!

'Coward,' she muttered to herself, pouring herself yet another hot drink. Because that was the truth, wasn't it? Yes, she was busy, but that wasn't the real reason she hadn't nipped outside to say hello. The truth was, she simply didn't have the brain space to unpack what had happened between them. There would be plenty of time for all that when they'd both finished their work. She hoped.

Poor old Harry – there really did seem to be a lot of work left to do on the ferry. Patricia didn't really know very much about boats, but she guessed that it must be the case judging by the fact that the ferry was still upside down on her patch of the bank. That couldn't bode well, could it?

It didn't bother her, though. It wasn't like she was desperate to have her muddy stretch of riverbank back! She barely ever went out there even when the weather was nice – other than to occasionally hack the scrubby bushes back so they didn't completely obscure her view of the river. She strimmed the grass now and then to keep it under control, but other than that, she didn't really use it.

Patricia was more than happy to let the council carry on using it for as long as they liked – especially if it meant that she got to see Harry every day – even if it was from a distance!

Unable to stop herself, she shifted towards the window for a quick peek outside. She did this every now and again, as if taking little sips of Harry would sustain her through her work until she had time to really think about what had happened between the pair of them… and what it might mean.

'Aw damn,' she muttered. Harry was nowhere to be seen – but a couple of things had changed since she'd last rewarded herself with a glance through the window.

Harry had used the scrubby bushes and delicate silver birch trees to rig up a tarpaulin. It looked like it served as a pretty decent makeshift cover – and at least the poor guy finally had a little bit of shelter while he worked. She had to admit, she was impressed at the lengths he was going to in order to get the ferry running - especially with the weather being this bad. Patricia couldn't think of many other people who'd continue working outside in these conditions.

The ferry was still the wrong way up, but Harry had clearly hauled it further up the bank so that it was away from the swollen river's edge. The rain had been coming down consistently for more than a week now, and the Bamton was starting to flood – just beginning to test its usual boundaries here and there. It looked like it was still fairly sedate at the moment – but Patricia knew that could change rapidly when things got going. Thankfully, her house was well out of the danger zone as it had been built on a higher shelf of bedrock. The only flood she'd encountered in all the years she'd lived there was that stupid water tank destroying her studio.

Patricia had to admit that she was starting to consider that particular disaster in a slightly different light. If the leak hadn't happened, she would never have paused long enough to see that she had taken the wrong turn with her work. She would never have discovered this new direction that she was so excited about. Without the flood, she would probably have just pushed ahead and submitted her old designs – even though she'd never really been happy with them. Then where would she be?

It would have been bad enough if Butter hadn't liked them… but it would have been even worse if they *had!* Then she'd have been stuck having to come up with more of the same, and getting further and further away from what she really loved. That would have been soul-destroying.

It was definitely better this way… though it hadn't felt much like it at the time. It had taken Harry's help to look at it all a bit differently.

Patricia let out a long sigh and peered back outside,

just on the off-chance that he'd reappeared while she'd been mooning around, but no luck. All there was to see was the flapping tarpaulin and the rain, which was now beating steadily against the window.

In a way, she was glad to be stuck indoors where it was warm and dry, and all she had to do was listen to the rain while she worked her behind off.

She was too busy to get stir-crazy - but she had to admit that a good long bike ride would help blow away the cobwebs. Actually – scratch that – it would be a terrible idea! A ride on Wally might have been the kind of calm, restorative potter she was dreaming of – but knowing the new bike, it would simply be a recipe for grazed knees and maybe even a broken arm. Right now, that was the last thing she needed!

Without thinking, Patricia abandoned cup of coffee number seven on the draining board. Turning back to the kitchen, she made her way over to her armchair - it was time to settle in for the next knitting marathon.

CHAPTER 11

The day had dawned at long last. *The* day. Patricia had been up since four thirty – checking and re-checking the wheely case where she'd packed her precious sample garments. They were all nestled inside carefully-folded sheets of acid-free tissue paper.

The good news was, every single time she checked them over, she got a thrill of excitement. She'd done it – she'd created a collection that she was not only proud of – but that was also very much *her*.

The bad news was… it was still raining… and boy, the weather gods seemed to be taking their duties seriously! This was the kind of rain that her old nan had described as "coming down like stair rods". It hammered on the roof and against the windows, and there hadn't been a single moment's let-up in the three hours since she'd dragged herself out of bed.

The Bamton had now properly burst its banks, and from what she could see from her anxious lookout at the kitchen window, there were various bits of tree and random debris being brought downstream by the dull, brownish swirling water.

At least the ferry was no longer out there on the bank. Harry had dropped a note through her letterbox a couple of days ago to let her know that he'd taken it to get the engine mounted. In fact – he was due back with it today – though she very much doubted that he'd be able to get it in the water when he turned up – not with the weather like this.

The journey up to London was going to be a rough one, that was for sure. Patricia was intensely grateful that she'd thought to book her train ticket in advance – at least it meant that she wouldn't have to stand all the way there like she'd had to in the past. She also had a taxi booked to get her to the station in plenty of time… now all that was left to do was fight the urge to open, check and re-pack her cases for the umpteenth time.

In a bid to stop her brain from obsessing about how the meeting would go, she flicked on the radio, followed by the kettle. Perhaps the usual inane chatter of the local station would settle her thoughts long enough for her to actually get an entire cup of coffee into her system.

Two seconds later, she switched the kettle back off again. The travel news had just started, and Patricia felt her stomach clench with fear.

"...a landslide on the tracks will mean that all trains will be cancelled. This is likely to continue to be the case for several days until it is safe for work crews to begin clearing the tracks and shoring the bank."

'Where?' demanded Patricia. She'd missed which stretch of the line was affected, but the newsreader had already moved on.

'Okay, okay, don't panic,' she muttered. It could be anywhere in the county. With any luck, it would be further down towards Cornwall, and wouldn't impact her journey at all. Ha - if only! With her luck, it was a fair bet that her train would be one of the ones that were cancelled.

Patricia legged it upstairs in search of her mobile, which she'd left charging. Sitting on the edge of her bed, she quickly searched for the local news pages.

'Come on you stupid thing, load!' she muttered as she watched a little circle going around and around on the screen. She'd been meaning to upgrade her phone forever, but she barely ever used the thing, so there didn't seem to be much point.

At long last, the page loaded and she scrolled down to the story.

'Aw no!' Patricia. She scanned the words three times and then tossed her phone away from her. Sure enough, her train was cancelled.

'Okay, okay... don't panic.'

The self-pep-talk wasn't working. Her nerves about

the day had just morphed into unadulterated, pounding worry. This was a complete disaster.

She'd already delayed this meeting once… she couldn't do it again. That would make her come across as totally unreliable, and she knew in her heart that it would ruin the relationship between her and Butter forever.

Besides, she didn't *want* to miss this meeting. She'd worked her backside off getting ready for it and she was proud of what she'd achieved. She'd simply have to come up with an alternative plan to get to London, that was all.

Patricia covered her eyes with her hands and slumped back onto her duvet, trying to rally her anxious thoughts into something a bit more useful than *"doooooooooooom!"* It was proving to be harder than expected.

It was on days like this she wished she'd bothered to learn how to drive. Then again – with the weather misbehaving quite so thoroughly, even if she had learned, she wasn't sure she'd have had the nerve to drive herself all the way up to London, only to have to face navigating the city streets at the other end!

Of course, if she could drive she could just run herself over to Dunscombe Sands. That would be the simple answer to this problem.

Patricia sat bolt upright. Of course! There was the slow train that left from Dunscombe. It followed a different route and took forever to get up to London because it stopped at every single wooden bus stop masquerading as a train station on the way. On the bright side though, it *would* miss the landslide completely.

Patricia grabbed her phone again and checked the time. She'd need to get over to Dunscombe pretty sharpish if she was to have any hope in hell of making it to her meeting in time.

She quickly checked that the slow train was still running – and breathed a sigh of relief. She was in luck.

Pulling up the number for the taxi company, Patricia crossed her fingers as she listened to it ring.

'Bamton Taxis, Chris speaking.'

'Hey Chris, it's Patricia Woodley here at River Cottage in Bamton Ford.'

'Hello love – don't worry – you're all pencilled in for later,' came the cheery response.

'Bit of a problem,' said Patricia, her voice quivering slightly, 'my train's been cancelled.'

'Ah – I heard something about a landslide?' came Chris's voice, slightly crackly now. She could hear road noise on the other end – he must be out somewhere on a fare. She could only hope he was somewhere local! 'So – do you need to cancel?'

'I was wondering if you might be able to take me down to Dunscombe Sands instead?'

'At the same time?' said Chris.

'Actually – as soon as you can make it over to me,' said Patricia.

'I could probably manage ten minutes sooner than you're booked in, but I'm on my way up towards Bristol right now – and in this weather, I won't be back much before it's time to pick you up.'

'Ah... okay...'

'I'm really sorry. Maybe you can find someone to give you a lift?'

Patricia nodded. That might not be such a bad idea. 'I'll text you to let you know if I manage it?'

'Right you are love – as long as I know if you still need me by the time I'm due at yours, I'm happy.'

'Great. Thanks Chris. Safe travels.'

'You too love. Good luck!'

Patricia hung up and stared at the silent phone in her hand for a few seconds. Right... she had a couple of options left. She could somehow strap everything onto her bicycle and ride down to Dunscombe Sands. But frankly, that was the worst idea she'd ever had in her entire life.

It was quite a long way to Dunscombe Sands. On top of that, she wasn't one hundred per cent sure of the directions and she had a fair amount of stuff she needed to take with her to London for the presentation - including the patterns, sample garments and her overnight bag. The new bike didn't even have a basket – and she was pretty sure that the useless thing would dump her in a ditch before she'd even made it to the other side of Upper Bamton. Even if she did manage to stay in the saddle, there was no way she could ride all that way with her gear slung across her back in this weather and make it all the way there in one piece.

The other option was Harry. She wondered if he'd be willing to give her a lift over to Dunscombe when he arrived - that would solve the problem. Sure, it might be a bit awkward given that they hadn't even spoken to each other since he'd handed his grandmother's jumpers over. But frankly, getting to this meeting on time would be worth a bit of awkwardness.

Right... she'd do it... she'd ask Harry for his help. If he didn't turn up in the next half an hour, she'd call James and ask him for Harry's number.

Patricia unplugged her phone and charger and hurtled back down the stairs. Heading into the kitchen, she proceeded to stand by the sink and watch the rain-splattered riverbank, obsessively keeping an eye out for Harry's arrival.

After five minutes, she was an anxious mess. Surely he was going to turn up? He wouldn't let a bit of extra rain put him off, would he? After ten minutes, she'd started to double-guess whether he'd even agree to help her when he *did* finally arrive. After all – they still hadn't talked about their... erm... *moment*. Okay, so it had been more than just a moment. A *lot* more than just a moment...

Patricia had stuck firm with the belief that they'd just been giving each other space to get on with their respective projects, and that they'd discuss what had happened between them after her deadline had passed and Harry had the ferry back in the water. But what if that wasn't the case? What if he'd had a horrible time? What if she'd pounced on him with no warning and he'd just been too polite to tell her to stop?

'Gah!!'

Patricia started to pace the kitchen. She was going to drive herself mad at this rate. She couldn't think about all *that* right now. She had to focus on her meeting... that's if she ever got there. She'd untangle the whole mess with Harry when she got back.

At the twenty-minute mark, she was just about to explode when she heard a lot of rattling and the sound of crunching tyres. She rushed to the front door only to find a very muddy, slightly beaten up old Discovery right outside that she'd never seen before. Behind it, the ferry was strapped to its wheels and proudly bearing its new engine.

'Hi Patricia,' said Harry, his head appearing on the other side as he unfolded himself from the car.

'Harry!' she said, cursing herself for blushing at the sight of him and the ridiculously breathy voice that had just escaped her. She cleared her throat.

'I need to talk to you,' said Harry, making his way straight for her and taking her by surprise.

Uh oh!

'I... erm... Harry, I know that we need to talk and

everything after the other day, but I've got a bit of an emergency going on. The trains-'

'Have been cancelled,' said Harry, nodding. 'Yes – I know – that's what I was on my way to tell you. I know it's your meeting today up in London but-'

'Right!' said Patricia, cutting him off in her embarrassment. She couldn't believe he'd actually remembered that it was today. She cleared her throat again. 'About the other thing...'

'We'll talk about that when you get back?'

Patricia nodded awkwardly. 'Great – I was going to ask-'

'I was coming to-'

The pair of them talked over each other and then laughed uncomfortably.

'You go,' said Harry with a smile.

'I need to ask you a favour. Would you mind giving me a lift over to Dunscombe Sands so that I can catch the slow train instead? If I go now I might be able to... what?' she paused, staring. Harry was shaking his head.

'That's what I was going to tell you... there's no way out of here by road now either. The way out through Upper Bamton - past the vineyard - is blocked by a fallen tree. I just about managed to get through by driving over the corner of someone's field, and the trailer almost got bogged down in the mud. It's going to be pretty much impassable by now I should imagine. I wouldn't risk even trying it again – if we got stuck, it would be a hell of a long walk back!'

'What about the lower road?' said Patricia, her heart sinking.

Harry shook his head again. 'The river's burst its banks. It's flooded and it's only going to get worse. And they're not even going to try to clear that tree today with the weather like it is… so we're kind of stranded. I was going to ask if you'd mind if I stayed here this evening?'

Patricia's eyebrows flew up.

'On the sofa,' he added quickly.

'Of course,' she said faintly. 'That's fine.'

She barely took in his murmured thanks. Her mind was frantically searching for any other options that might get her to her meeting on time. She'd never been marooned before. Normally, it wouldn't bother her in the slightest, but today she just felt desperate - she *needed* to get to London.

There was no way she could walk all that way to Dunscombe with her stuff – even on a good day. Maybe Harry could drive her as far as the fallen tree… she could trudge with her stuff through the muddy field to the other side and… and then what?

She stared at Harry's car again… not *quite* the saviour she'd been hoping for. Then her eyes drifted towards the ferry.

'Harry?'

'Yeah?' he said, following her gaze.

'How close is the ferry to being back in the water?'

'It's all done and ready to go! Ohhhh no,' he said,

shaking his head. 'Nope nope nope. It's about ten miles from here down the river to Dunscombe Sands.'

'But... theoretically, it's doable?' she asked.

'Theoretically,' he chuckled. 'But have you seen the river today?'

'A bit fuller than usual,' said Patricia with a little shrug. 'But don't you need to test out that engine anyway?'

Harry sighed. 'I do, yes.'

He paused and Patricia could see that he was considering things. She stayed quiet, her fingers crossed behind her back.

'Right,' he said at last. 'Here's the deal. I'll take you. We should be okay as long as we're careful – but you have to do exactly what I say. If I think it's too dangerous at any point, we're heading straight for the bank and back to safety – with *no* arguments. Deal?'

Patricia nodded, grinning at him. 'Deal.'

'And you have to wear a life jacket.'

Patricia nodded again. 'Glamorous,' she sighed.

'Not half as glamorous as that hat you were wearing the first day we met!' laughed Harry.

CHAPTER 12

'More tape around this bit, I reckon?' said Harry.

Patricia nodded and started to wrap a long line of noisy parcel tape around the bin bag that was covering the case holding her precious samples, while Harry held it steady for her.

He'd been the one to suggest covering all her things in plastic for their protection during their journey down the river. Patricia had readily agreed – grateful to him for being so thoughtful. She knew the bin bags weren't exactly glamorous and would do absolutely nothing to protect her stuff should anything fall into the swirling waters of the Bamton, but they would stop every little splash from signalling potential disaster.

Harry had already wheeled the ferry down the slip. With some difficulty, he'd got her in the water. The little boat was now tied securely to the bank, waiting for them to begin their hair-brained adventure. According to Harry, the river was running higher than ever and the rain had decided to renew its efforts while Patricia had been busy gathering the last few bits and pieces for their journey. For one horrible moment, she'd thought he was about to call the whole plan off.

'As long as we go carefully, I'm pretty confident we'll be fine. The river up here at Bamton Ford is nice and wide and slow – even in this weather, it's much more gentle than a bit further down – so at least it'll give us a good start,' he laughed, helping her with her newly-wrapped bags.

'You sound like you know the river pretty well?' said Patricia in surprise.

'Yup – there's nothing quite like pottering up and down the Bamton in a boat – I love it! Though I tend to start out down near Seabury.'

'Is that where you live?' she asked.

'Just outside,' he said with a little shrug. 'I'm between there and Bucklepool at the moment. Though I've got a feeling I'm going to be spending a lot more time up here now...'

He trailed away, catching Patricia's eye, and they both froze in the hallway. Patricia let out a soft hum. As much as she'd like to jump on Harry just as she'd done the other day – there simply wasn't time!

'I mean with the ferry,' he clarified quickly.

'Sure, sure,' said Patricia, nodding quickly. 'And babysitting duties, no doubt?'

'Hmm... I might do my best to avoid those until the little miss is at least at the toddling stage.'

'Coward,' laughed Patricia.

'You'd better believe it,' said Harry, nodding. 'Now – let's get these loaded up – and then you'd better get dressed.'

'I'm already dressed,' laughed Patricia, following him through the open front door and ducking her head as huge rain drops instantly started splattering down onto her face.

'You'll see what I mean,' chuckled Harry, giving her a wink.

It didn't take them long to secure her cases in the boat – with Patricia passing them from the bank down to Harry, who carefully stashed them on board. As soon as he was back on dry land, Harry led her back up the bank to his Discovery. He rummaged around in the back for a few minutes, only to emerge brandishing a set of waterproofs, some oversized wellington boots and a lifejacket.

'Lucky you brought the lifejackets with you!' said Patricia.

Harry shrugged. 'I brought them over so that they're ready for the passengers when I get the ferry on the go. Everyone has to wear one.'

Patricia nodded. James had always insisted on the same thing. She wasn't sure if it was a council requirement or not, but it was definitely common sense... especially given how idiotic some of the visitors seemed to be the minute they set foot on the little boat!

'I'll take the waterproofs and the lifejacket,' said Patricia, pulling a face, 'but these wellies are absolutely massive!'

'Better than nothing,' said Harry.

'They would be... but I think I'll wear my own, thanks!'

'I like a woman with her own wellies,' chuckled Harry, wiggling his eyebrows at her.

Patricia froze as a tingle of pure longing ran down her spine. Crikey! At this rate, it wouldn't be the weather stopping her from getting to London, but the fact that she was too busy dragging Harry back to her lair!

'Go on,' chuckled the troublemaker in question, clearly catching the look of pure lust that she was shooting in his direction. 'Get dressed and let's get this moment of insanity underway – before we both decide we've got something better to do!'

Two minutes later, Patricia was fully togged up in waterproofs, wellies, hat and lifejacket. She'd managed to calm herself down and was now standing on the bank, feeling like a total lemon. She looked almost as bad as she had done the first time she'd run into Harry. At least this time, she was actually heading out onto the river on purpose!

Now she was standing here, waiting for Harry to give her a hand to climb aboard, she couldn't help but stare at the swollen river. Its murky water had a decidedly ominous look about it, and she felt her nerve begin to fade a little bit. Still, this had to be better than trying to cycle through a flood or around fallen trees on that stupid bike, didn't it? At least this way there was a slim chance that she might actually make it to her destination intact.

'Ready?' called Harry. He was already pottering around on the ferry, looking as sure-footed as a mountain goat… an aquatic mountain goat.

Patricia swallowed her nerves and nodded. Harry grinned and held out his hand for her to take. She did so gratefully, squeezing his fingers rather harder than was strictly necessary as she navigated her way off the slippery bank and into the boat. Blimey, this lifejacket made it feel like she was trying to manoeuvre whilst wearing a sumo suit!

'Thanks,' she said, her voice sounding more than a little bit strangled as she sank down onto a seat. Her knees didn't feel particularly trustworthy all of a sudden.

'Right then – here goes nothing!' said Harry, pushing them away from the bank.

As he started up the engine, Patricia fought the urge to beg to be allowed back onto dry land, and instead, wrapped her fingers tightly around the edges of her seat. She could practically feel her knuckles turning white. She certainly *hoped* they'd reach Dunscombe Sands safely! Whatever else happened, it looked like this was going to be a memorable trip... she just hoped that it would be for the right reasons!

Patricia peered around fearfully as they made their way out towards the middle of the river. Hadn't Harry told her that this stretch of the river was one of the calmest? If that was the case, there certainly seemed to be an awful lot of current out here... as well as... what was that?!

'That's a-'

'Plastic garden chair?' said Harry. 'Yup! I expect we'll see plenty more of that sort of thing before we reach Dunscombe. Apparently, further upstream, the river is washing through people's back gardens!'

Patricia widened her eyes in horror, and then went back to staring at the water. It didn't take long before Harry was proved right. The chair sighting was joined by a whole bunch of random objects being carried along, caught up in the swift-flowing torrent. There was a garden shed that tumbled in the water, one minute showing its roof, the next its door. A bird table appeared right next to the boat, followed by a plastic sundial and then half a dozen plastic flower pots – all floating along like a row of bobbing ducklings.

The most eery sighting was a pair of wellington boots that swept past them, bobbing along upside down as if the wearer was underwater.

'Do you think-?' she gasped.

'No,' said Harry, looking horrified. He'd clearly been

thinking exactly the same thing. 'No,' he said again, 'definitely not.'

Patricia's house was far behind them before she allowed herself to ease her death grip on her seat. She let out a long, slow breath, willing herself to relax a bit. At this rate, she'd be stiff as a board by the time she reached the train station – her nerves would be shot before she'd even had the chance to start worrying about how the meeting would pan out.

Harry certainly seemed to know what he was doing, and considering how rough the river was, there hadn't been a single second when it felt like he wasn't in control.

'The engine's doing well,' she said. 'I'm guessing, if it can handle this, it'll be able to handle anything?'

Harry shot her a grin. 'I have to admit, I was quite surprised when it actually fired up first time!'

'You were?' said Patricia

'Absolutely,' said Harry, 'it's been languishing in James's garage all winter - and I don't think it's had much in the way of TLC and maintenance if I'm honest.'

'But it's safe?' she squeaked, the fear returning.

'It might conk out halfway down the river,' he chuckled, 'but frankly, that wouldn't be a problem today, the river would take us all the way to Dunscombe Sands with no problem. We probably wouldn't even notice the difference other than it being a bit more peaceful!' Then he clearly clocked her anxious look, because he quickly added, 'I'm sure it'll be fine!'

Patricia really wanted to believe him, but even so, she kept an ear out for any signs of spluttering coming from the engine.

It really was quite beautiful out here on the river. If there wasn't so much resting on this journey, she might have been able to relax and let herself enjoy the lush, wet, leafy banks as they sped by. The way the fat raindrops created ripples on the surface of the river was mesmerising. It was really quite magical - or it would be if they weren't in such a hurry!

Maybe, when she got back and the weather cheered up a bit she could convince Harry to take her out on a private ferry ride... they could take a picnic... maybe discover a private little stretch of bank and...

'What's happened?' she demanded. The river was incredibly wide by this point. She'd suddenly noticed that they were getting closer and closer to the left bank. 'What's the problem? Is everything okay?'

'Calm down!' Harry laughed, smiling at her kindly and shaking his head in amusement. 'We're nearly there.'

'Where?' demanded Patricia.

'Dunscombe Sands, you lunatic,' laughed Harry. 'We're not far from the harbour mouth.'

'Already?' she said in surprise.

Harry nodded and pointed.

Patricia turned to see Bamton Boatyard glide by,

with its motley collection of huge, knackered boats, most of them awaiting some serious maintenance by the looks of things.

'Blimey - that didn't take long!' she said.

'Well - we had extra river power behind us today!' laughed Harry. 'If we hurry when we get there, you might even make the next train.'

Patricia nodded in excitement, and a surge of nerves ran through her. Was she really going to make it after all? It was pretty hard to believe it after everything that had happened that morning.

For a while there, it had felt like all the long hours of work - all those early mornings and late nights – were going to be wasted. Now, thanks to Harry, it looked like everything was going to be okay.

Patricia started to breathe out a long sigh of relief... and then stopped herself short. She didn't want to jinx it before she was actually on that train, and it had set off!

As Harry steered the little ferry into the mouth of Dunscombe Sands harbour, Patricia couldn't pretend that there wasn't a part of her that wanted to stay here with him on the boat. Now that it was nearly over, she had to admit that she'd thoroughly enjoyed their mad adventure down the river. With any luck, there would be time for plenty more adventures together when she got back home.

CHAPTER 13

Patricia stood at the top of the stone steps, relishing how stable and solid the harbour wall felt under her feet after their mad, rocking dash down the river. Harry was busy below, making sure that the little boat was tied up safely. By some kind of miracle, they'd arrived in Dunscombe Sands harbour – and all three of them seemed to be in one piece – her, Harry and the ferry!

'There – that should do it,' said Harry, smiling up at her and laughing as he instantly had to wipe raindrops from his face.

'Right. Excellent,' said Patricia. 'Thank you so much... for everything. I'd better grab my cases and make a dash for it if I'm going to catch this train!'

'Don't be daft!' said Harry, hefting the heaviest of the cases onto the steps and dragging it up to the top.

He came to a standstill in front of her. 'I'll help you get your stuff to the station.'

Patricia stared at him, losing herself for a moment in his hazel, green-flecked eyes. 'Thank you,' she croaked. She quickly cleared her throat. Now was not the time for all the mushy stuff – hadn't she promised herself to put all that firmly to the back of her mind until she came home?!

Following Harry back down the steps, watched him hop back onto the ferry and then quickly moved forward to grab her bags as he handed them over the side.

'Ready?' said Harry, following her back to the top of the steps and promptly wresting the handle of the heaviest case back out of her hand.

Patricia grinned. She'd let him win that one! She threw the bag containing her change of clothes over her shoulder – at least she wouldn't have to travel all the way to London looking like a badly put-together fisherman – then quickly scanned the back of the boat one last time to make sure they had everything. After all this effort, she didn't want to end up in the meeting only to discover that she'd left a key ingredient behind on the ferry!

'Okay... ready!' she said with a determined nod.

The pair of them hurtled along the rain-soaked harbour front, and then Harry led her down a side street.

Patricia started to pant as she jogged along, her

wellington boots slapping against the paving stones. She was so thankful that Harry had insisted on coming all the way to the station with her – Dunscombe was a maze of side streets and alley-ways.

'Are you sure this is the way?' she puffed, following Harry as he jogged slightly ahead of her.

'Short cut!' he called over his shoulder.

Sure enough, two seconds later, they scooted around a corner only to come face to face with the little white building that was Dunscombe Sands station.

They both hurtled straight onto the platform and then skidded to a halt. They'd only just made it in time – the train bound for London was sitting on the tracks as though it had been waiting for them, and the guard was checking his watch.

'Quick!' said Harry, ushering Patricia towards the nearest door. The train was absolutely minuscule but - from what she could see through the windows - it looked mercifully quiet. She scrambled on board and Harry handed her case up to her.

'Thanks!' she puffed, taking it from him.

Turning to the little vestibule, she dumped everything onto the floor - only to hear the door slam behind her and the engines start to gear up.

Straightening back up, Patricia quickly turned around again and yanked down the window, a sudden worry forming in her nervous brain.

'How are you going to get back?' she gasped, trying

to catch her breath now that she was safely on board. 'Surely there's no way the ferry will make it back up the river against the flow?'

Harry shook his head. 'You're right. Don't worry, I'll grab a bus over to Seabury and stay in the hotel tonight – then maybe try my luck getting back home tomorrow.'

Patricia nodded, then jolted as the train began to move.

'Thanks, Harry!' she said, waving at him.

'Good luck!' he shouted, 'Make sure you…'

But whatever it was she needed to make sure of, she didn't catch. The train was moving away and she couldn't hear him over the noise. Instead, she waved frantically, grinning as she watched him wave back. A huge smile spread over his lovely face before he disappeared as a curtain of rain fell between them.

Patricia drew back inside the train and pulled the window up with a dull thud. It was time to find somewhere to stash all her things and then find a seat. Oh – and change out of her ridiculous clothes too! She glanced down at the lifejacket she was still wearing and laughed.

'You're on a train now, you know,' said a bemused conductor as he appeared through the doorway to the next carriage. 'I don't think you'll be needing that – unless you know something I don't!'

Patricia glanced down at the life vest again and then grinned at him.

'Can I buy a ticket, please? Bit of a change of plans this morning.'

'Because of the landslide?' he asked, raising his eyebrows.

Patricia nodded.

'You go ahead and get yourself comfy – find a seat and I'll be back along in a minute. Just be sure not to float away while I'm gone… deal?'

'Deal,' she laughed, watching in amusement as he toddled off down the aisle. Someone with a sense of humour? Perfect! That was just what she needed to calm her nerves after that mad dash.

Reaching behind her, Patricia started to wrestle with the knots so that she could remove the bulky lifejacket.

Now that she was safe and sound on board the train, the insanity of what the pair of them had just done was starting to sink in. What on earth had she been thinking? She could so easily have made a phone call to Butter and postponed the meeting again. At the time, with her anxiety at its peak, it had felt like a disastrous thing to do… but now she could see that, in reality, it wouldn't have been the end of the world.

Ah well – here she was, on the train in one piece. If she *had* called and cancelled her meeting, she'd have missed out on that mad adventure with Harry! Yes, it had been scary and exciting – and more than a little bit stupid - but she couldn't remember the last time she'd had so much fun. It had been like something straight out of a film!

Patricia finally managed to get the knots undone and pulled the lifejacket over her head. That was *definitely* better! Considering the soggy combination of the river and the rain, she wasn't even really that wet!

Patricia picked up one of her bags and hauled it through into the carriage, stashing it along with the bulky lifejacket on one of the overhead racks. Then she went back for the rest. As soon as she'd got everything neatly tucked away, she decided that it was time to find the loo and change into some normal-person clothes. As exciting as it had been to dash around in a pair of wellies, now she was craving warm, cosy and dry!

There was one thing she still couldn't wrap her head around from this whole bizarre morning. Why on earth had Harry agreed to give her hair-brained idea a go? He'd said yes to hurtling down a flooded river in a newly-repaired boat sporting an untested engine. Clearly, the guy was as nuts as she was. Patricia smiled to herself... that had to bode well, didn't it?!

A warm sensation ran through her that had nothing to do with the extra layer of waterproof clothing, and everything to do with the slightly rugged stranger she'd just left behind on the platform edge. Mind you, she couldn't really call him a stranger anymore, could she? Harry now held prime position in most of her waking thoughts... and it was best not to think too much about her night-time thoughts!

Patricia wrapped her fingers around the back of one of the seats as the little train lurched around a corner. Her fingers felt sore from gripping on for dear life all the way down the river. It was a miracle that the little ferry had made it in one piece. She wasn't really sure how many repairs Harry had done over the past few days. From her vantage point at the cottage's front window, most of them had seemed to be fairly superficial – sanding, filling holes and varnishing – but what did she know?

They could have sprung a leak halfway down the river and sunk... or capsized... or the motor could have conked out – just like Harry had warned her it might.

Patricia shook her head slightly as she continued to make her way down the carriage. Harry was clearly too well practised at navigating the river to let anything actually cause them any harm. Then again, there was no way he could have accounted for all of the rubbish they'd encountered on the way down towards Dunscombe Sands. They could have so easily run into a floating shed...

Ah well – there was no point worrying about it now, was there? Though, she might owe Harry yet another apology for even suggesting such a nutty plan when she returned home.

There was one thing she could say with all certainty about the whole affair – it had been a lot more exciting than sitting in a taxi and being driven to the station!

The train lurched again and Patricia swore lightly

under her breath. Every jolt seemed to give her nerves another little poke. There was no doubt about it – she felt a bit like that garden shed in the river! She was busy hurtling downstream – swirling her around and around until she didn't know which way was up.

Taking a deep breath, Patricia decided that – for now, at least – she just had to let the river take her. Yanking open the door to the little toilet, she disappeared inside.

When Patricia emerged a couple of minutes later, she felt more human again. Making her way back along the carriage, she stuffed the wet-weather gear and her wellies onto the rack with the rest of her things. Then, she quickly counted her bags so that she wouldn't forget anything when she changed trains, and found herself a cosy window seat.

Snuggling down, Patricia turned to watch as the rain-drenched summer landscape swept past the windows. A huge, warm, satisfied smile spread across her face - at long last, she could just relax and enjoy the journey. Whatever happened next was fine by her... she was just happy to be along for the ride.

'Righty-ho!' said the conductor, appearing at her side with a cheery grin. 'Glad to see you haven't been washed away.'

Patricia smiled up at him, feeling at peace with the world.

CHAPTER 14

It was proving hard not to skip down the busy London street. Every couple of steps, Patricia gave a funny little shuffle-step of pure delight, gaining disapproving glances from the work-weary commuters around her. Frankly – she didn't care. The meeting with Butter had been… she didn't even have the words to describe how incredible it had been.

As soon as the conductor had helped her to work out exactly what time her train would be arriving at Paddington, Patricia had pulled her big-girl pants on and called Jade, her main contact at Butter. She had a problem. Even though she'd be arriving in London in plenty of time for the meeting, she'd need to navigate all the way across the city to get to Butter's offices. The chances of her managing to do this before the meeting was due to begin were… slim!

As it happened – Jade turned out to be one of those people who seemed to be able to fix anything. Ten minutes after she'd hung up, a message pinged onto Patricia's phone to tell her that there would be a private car waiting to pick her up at Paddington. It would whisk her straight to the Butter offices, and then drop her luggage at her hotel so that she wouldn't have to deal with it afterwards.

The result of all this hospitable efficiency had been that Patricia had arrived for the meeting feeling rested, unruffled and vaguely coherent, rather than hot, sweaty and late.

And then... the whole thing had been better than she could have ever dreamed. Jade and her creative team – Raif and Manuel - turned out to be just as friendly and open in person as they had been by email and phone. Even more importantly – at least as far as Patricia was concerned – they loved her designs.

According to them, she'd hit the nail on the head with the collection. They'd thrown words like *classic* and *unpretentious* and *authentic* around like confetti.

In fact, they'd been so impressed that they'd immediately commissioned more work from her. Two more collections with twice the number of designs. It was the kind of contract that dreams were made of, and Patricia had to work pretty hard to keep her cool, professional head on her shoulders instead of squealing and hugging everyone on the spot. But then, as soon as she'd given them verbal confirmation that she'd *love* to keep working with them, Jade had squealed, Manuel had hugged her and Raif had popped a bottle of bubbly that seemed to appear from nowhere.

Patricia grinned at her reflection as she strode passed a coffee shop window and then realised that she was probably scaring the teenagers sitting at the window table. Ah well! Nothing could puncture her good mood right now. She couldn't believe that she got to work with this amazing company – and that they were just as excited to work with her. This new contract would keep her busy for the rest of the year – and a good chunk of next year too.

The meeting couldn't have gone any better… and to think – just this morning it had looked like she might not even be able to make it! Patricia had decided to spare them all the gory details of her rather unusual adventure getting there. They knew she'd had to swap trains, but they didn't really need to know the ins and outs of her mad dash down the river with Harry. These people, lovely as they were, were alarmingly stylish and cutting edge. They probably all lived in converted wharf apartments on the Thames, but that was about as far as the river connection went. London felt weirdly cut off from the torrential rain and flooded Bamton she'd left behind her just that morning!

She pulled in a deep, excited breath. The moment she'd agreed to remain in London an extra few days,

Jade had got straight on the phone to extend her stay in the swanky hotel they were treating her to. There would be more meetings to discuss the finer details of the new collections... and Patricia was already looking forward to it. Right now, though, with the first meeting done and dusted, she was rather looking forward to reaching the hotel, changing into something comfy and over-ordering on the room service.

Jade had offered to have her driven back to the hotel, but Patricia had opted to walk instead. She'd left the heavy case full of sketches, patterns and samples in the office, and had thoroughly enjoyed blowing off a little bit of steam with her little shuffle-hops on her way to the hotel.

And there it was in front of her – five floors of pure class – its subtle, expensive white and dove grey frontage practically glowing in the soft evening light.

After taking a moment to gawp - and then to marvel at Butter's generosity in putting her up in such a gorgeous place - Patricia trotted up the marble staircase, her hand trailing along the polished brass handrail as she went.

The moment she stepped into the foyer, a man wearing an exquisite three-piece suit stepped out from behind a desk and approached her with a smile.

'Good evening. Welcome to the Em Dash Hotel!'

'Thanks!' said Patricia, slightly taken aback and fighting the strange urge to bow for some reason.

'Erm... I've got a room booked for the next three nights... it might be under "Butter"?'

'Ah – Ms Woodley?'

Patricia nodded. Was this man magic?

'That's right, your luggage arrived earlier. Your bags are already in your room, but I took the liberty of sending your lifejacket and waterproofs down to the laundry so that they could be dried out properly. I hope that's acceptable?'

'That's... that's really kind!' she said, smiling at him broadly. This guy was pure class. Just the fact that he'd called her bedraggled, bin-liner-wrapped bags "luggage" went to prove it.

'It was my pleasure. Now, let me escort you up to your room.'

Patricia shook her head. 'There's really no need – thank you!' She'd feel awful trailing all the way there behind him.

'Very well. Here is your key card, and if you need anything at all, don't hesitate to dial zero on your phone.'

He handed a posh little leather wallet over to her that had a single dash printed in gold on the front. Snazzy!

'Will you be joining us for dinner this evening?' he asked.

Patricia shook her head. 'I was wondering if I might be able to order room service?'

'Of course. There's a full menu in the welcome pack – room service is available twenty-four hours a day.'

Patricia mumbled her thanks and made a bee-line for the stairs. It was official – this place was awesome. As she climbed the circular staircase, being careful not to trip on the plush carpet as she eyed the amazing light sculpture that dangled down all the way from the fifth floor, her thoughts flew back to Devon... and Harry.

He'd been popping up in her head every few minutes all day. He *was* her muse, after all! Now all she wanted to do was to contact him and tell him that – thanks to him - she'd managed to get here on time. Harry was the one person she wanted to share her amazing news with... what did that mean?

No matter how much she wanted to talk to Harry, she had no way of actually reaching him. She didn't have his number. She *did* have James's number – but that was pinned on the front of her fridge back home... so - not exactly helpful!

It didn't stop her burning desire to hear his voice, though. She wanted to know how he was... and whether the hotel in Seabury was anything like this one. Maybe they could even compare room service menus or something.

Patricia really hoped that they hadn't managed to harm the ferry on the way down the river. It would be entirely her fault if the engine had some kind of flower-pot-related damage going on. She'd definitely had to ask him when she got back – and offer to pay for the repairs if that was the case.

Patricia sighed with relief as she reached her room door. She paused, fiddling around with the little wallet and extracting the key card. She hated these blasted things – even when they were in posh little leather pouches!

At last, she let herself into the room and eyed the pristine Egyptian Cotton covered bed.

Oh hello!

Chucking her handbag onto the vanity table, she suddenly realised just how tired she was after today's excitement. She was glad now that she'd decided to come back here rather than find somewhere to eat on her way home. At least here she could change into her PJs, snuggle up on that marshmallowy bed and binge-watch some trashy TV. Maybe that would take her mind off the fact that it was going to be a couple of days before she'd get to see Harry again.

Patricia reached for the remote and flicked it on, channel hopping until she landed on *Casablanca*. Bingo! Not trashy at all – just perfect! She kicked off her shoes and climbed onto the bed, preparing to get nicely square-eyed.

The film didn't keep her attention for very long though. Patricia felt fidgety. She was used to spending time on her own – and normally, she preferred it – but not tonight. Her good news was swirling around inside her, mixing with images of Harry as he rushed her down the flooded river. Everything she'd achieved was down to him...

Designing a collection she loved...

Getting up here to present it on time...

Getting the chance to work with Butter for two more collections...

This was Harry's win as much as it was hers... and she couldn't even tell him about it.

Patricia sighed, plumped up the vast pile of pillows and threw herself back onto them. She was determined to relax and have a good time.

Two seconds later, her thoughts were back with Harry again. Not for the first time, she wondered what he did for a living. She was pretty sure that operating the Bamton ferry couldn't pay very much – just a small stipend from the council as far as she knew. In fact, James had once told her that he also worked as some kind of mechanic.

The passengers' fares for the ferry all went towards the upkeep of the Bamton Abbey site on the other side of the river – and the archaeological fund to help support the university's dig site. They hadn't actually found anything interesting there for years, though. All the good bits had been excavated and carted away to a museum sometime back in the 1950s. The team from the local university were always hopeful that something might show up that proved to be historically significant – but in the meantime, the site provided them with the ideal training ground. Gangs of students were regularly to be found there, working on their little trenches.

If she was being honest, Patricia was of the strong opinion that they all just enjoyed being taken across the river by James. A day out scraping away tiny patches of dirt with their dainty trowels had to be better than sitting in a stuffy lecture hall, didn't it?!

Patricia had gone over there to watch them once, but if she was being honest, it wasn't her sort of thing. She always thought they'd have much more luck poking around in the mud at the side of the river when the water was at its lowest. It regularly washed things out of the bank, and there were always shards of china, old bottles and all sorts of other goodies to be found in the silty mud.

She had a collection of finds in her house – all lined up along the windowsills. The colours of the glass – those wonderful greens and browns and the occasional piercing blue of an old poison bottle – were amazing inspiration for her knitting.

Come to think about it, she hadn't been out for a while now. Perhaps the flooded river would wash something new and exciting out of the bank. Maybe, when she got back, she'd ask Harry if he fancied accompanying her along the river bank… when the water had dropped, of course. That would be fun! Actually… she had plans to ask Harry lots of things. She had plenty of subjects in mind…

Patricia let her eyes drift closed. She'd just rest for a

few minutes, then she'd have a bath... order some room service... Just a couple of minutes on this cosy, soft bed with the traffic humming outside her hotel window was all she needed. It wasn't quite the same as listening to the river below her bedroom window – but it certainly had a similar effect.

With Harry's lovely smile lingering in the darkness behind her eyelids, Patricia drifted off to sleep.

CHAPTER 15

The last few days had disappeared in a whirlwind of meetings, inspiration, new designs and hastily knitted swatches. Patricia had even treated herself to a new sketchbook and had already begun to fill its pages with unusual ease.

She'd spent many wonderful hours discussing ideas and themes with the creative team at Butter - and felt like she'd made bonds there that she hoped would last a lifetime. It was a weird and unusual feeling to be treated like an artist – with both respect and playfulness – by people she respected so much in return.

The whole experience had definitely given her the gift of looking at her own work with renewed enthusiasm and - though she'd never admit it out loud to *anyone* – pride.

As much as she'd enjoyed every second of her London adventure, she had to admit that she was excited to be heading back to Devon. Patricia couldn't wait to get home to start bringing a whole new range of woolly creations to life.

That's not to say that saying goodbye to her gorgeous room at the Em Dash hadn't been a bit of a wrench. Staying in such luxury had been blissful. She'd made the most of the room service menu and had even strayed as far as the lovely in-house restaurant the previous evening.

Patricia had never had any qualms about enjoying a meal solo... it was perfect for people-watching. Normally she would have happily whiled away the entire evening, completely content with her own company. Last night though, every single moment had been tinged with a kind of wistful, frustrated melancholy... because Patricia had to admit that she was desperately missing Harry.

She found herself comparing every man in the place to him – searching for a similar pair of crinkling eyes with the distinctive emerald flashes. She'd even whipped around in her seat when she heard a laugh that – for a split second – had her heart hammering in her chest. For just a moment, she'd thought that perhaps Harry had arrived to surprise her. Stupid really... that kind of thing only happened in movies and books.

After finishing her meal, she'd decided to grab her sketchbook and go for a final wander along the Thames. She wanted to gather as many of the textures and colours of the river as possible so that she could weave them into her new designs. As she walked, Patricia had finally admitted something to herself... no matter how ridiculous it seemed because she'd only met Harry such a short while ago... she'd already fallen for him.

The realisation scared her senseless. Other than their adventure down the river together, and that memorable moment when she'd modelled her now-discarded designs for him, they didn't really know each other at all, did they?! Still, there would be plenty of time for all that when she got back home. It wouldn't be long now. It was just a matter of hours and she'd be back in Bamton Ford.

Patricia had her fingers crossed that everything at home would have survived the heavy rain. Thankfully, the worst of it seemed to be over. When she'd checked the weather forecast at breakfast, it looked like there were a couple of light showers over the south west this morning - and then it was due to clear up for a good few weeks.

Frankly, she'd believe that when she saw it, but she couldn't help but feel relieved at the prospect of a bit of sunshine to come. Patricia had plans for spending as much time outside as possible when she got back – mostly in Harry's company whenever he wasn't too busy. She was pretty sure she could talk him into it... even if it meant she had to slip into one of his jumpers and parade around without her trousers on for a bit.

That should do the trick... it had certainly worked its magic last time!

The great news was that while she'd been living it up in London, the mainline had reopened – so she wouldn't have to spend *quite* so many hours getting home. On top of that, when she'd finally been brave enough to regale Jade and the others with the full tale of her journey up to the capital, they'd insisted on forking out for a taxi to take her back to the station, and had even bumped her up to first class on the train.

Now, as she settled into her roomy, comfortable seat with her knitting needles in her hands, a huge smile spread over Patricia's face. Considering how difficult life had felt just a few days ago, it now seemed to be full of excitement, hope and even new purpose. She couldn't wait to pull all her little sketches and swatches together when she got home and start working on them in earnest. Funnily enough, rivers and rain seemed to be a key theme that was starting to shine through.

Who would have thought that Bamton Ford ferry of all things would bring someone like Harry into her life? It could have all ended in disaster so easily that first day when she'd been careening towards the river. Thank goodness he'd saved her. What if he'd missed and she'd gone in? What if he'd been the kind of person that might have missed on purpose only to stand on the bank laughing at her? Luckily, he'd proved that he was the complete opposite – warm, fun, chatty... and a little bit cheeky. She certainly knew exactly where James got that particular character trait from!

Patricia wondered how James and Mattie were getting on. Maybe when she got back, she'd get in touch and invite them over for a meal… along with Harry, of course. She didn't know much about babies, but she was sure the young couple could probably do with an evening out without having to cook. Of course, Harry wouldn't be available to babysit. Maybe they could just bring the little mite over with them.

She still couldn't quite wrap her head around the idea of Harry as a granddad. He was more like a big kid. His carefree attitude was strangely refreshing – and he clearly had a sense of adventure. She still couldn't put an age on him though. She was notoriously rubbish at guessing how old people were, but with Harry, she was completely lost. James had to be nearing thirty… so at a guess, maybe Harry was in his late forties or early fifties. Either way – who cared?

They had plenty of time to find out everything about each other. She had loads of things she wanted to share with Harry – and she was really excited to learn more about what made his world go around. For her, that was one of the best bits of a new relationship – that early sense of discovery.

Of course, she *might* be getting ahead of herself a bit by describing whatever was going on between them as a relationship. It was a bit early for all that… but… there *could* be something there, couldn't there?

Something prickled in the back of Patricia's mind. Suddenly, her plush chair felt less comfortable and her skin started to crawl. A thought had just popped into her head and in one horrible second, it managed to shatter her sense of serene excitement with a single axe blow.

What if this was all some kind of game to him? What if Harry was seeing someone else... or... oh God, what if he was married?! He *did* have James, after all. He didn't live in Upper Bamton, so she had no idea about his friends or his private life. It would have been so easy for him to just appear in her life, take advantage of her and then head back home to his wife, wouldn't it?!

How could she have been so stupid? She should have asked him outright the moment she'd met him.

Would this make it her fault if he *was* with someone? After all, she'd been the one to prance around in nothing but his jumper and then bare all as if she didn't have a care in the world! But no – she might be responsible for her own behaviour, but she wasn't responsible for his. That was on him!

Damnit, why wasn't this train faster? She needed to get back to Bamton Ford. Now. She suddenly had a whole load of questions for Harry – and they definitely wouldn't wait.

CHAPTER 16

The moment she stepped off the train, Patricia made a bee-line for the taxi rank, crossing her fingers that there would be one waiting. Just like her journey on the way up to London, she was in a hurry. Now wasn't the time to be catching the meandering bus back to Upper Bamton, only to have to walk the rest of the way back to Bamton Ford when she finally got there.

Throwing one bag over her shoulder, Patricia shoved the other one ahead of her on its little wheels. Two seconds later, she had to come to a screeching halt and fumble for her ticket at the turnstile to get out of the station. Eventually, the guard took pity on all her huffing and puffing – and opened the wider gate for her to walk through.

'You're an angel,' she said, shooting him a weary

smile as she manoeuvred past him with the stupid lifejacket tucked under her arm.

'My pleasure,' said the guard, eyeing it with curiosity, but clearly deciding that it was best *not* to make a joke – something she was intensely grateful for because she wasn't sure her response would have been particularly polite.

As it happened, luck was on her side, and there was a taxi sitting right outside the station as if it was waiting for her. Unfortunately, the driver didn't quite manage to gauge her mood as well as the guard had, and had a good chuckle as he loaded the lifejacket into the boot of the car.

'You look like you're preparing to load the animals two by two!' he laughed.

Patricia forced herself to smile at him. The man was only being friendly – and it wasn't his fault that she was heading back home to what might possibly be the most mortifying conversation of her entire life.

She let herself into the back seat of the car, hoping that it might deter the driver from small-talk all the way back to Bamton Ford. Unfortunately, she hadn't accounted for the fact that the guy had been bored out of his mind all morning and wanted to chat. Thankfully though, it didn't take very much input on her part other than the occasional nod, or murmur of agreement as he launched into a twenty-minute monologue on the recent bad weather, the state of the roads and the general uselessness of their local council.

The only problem with not really needing to engage with the driver was that by the time were trundling down the track towards her cottage, Patricia had managed to work herself up into a state. How on earth was she meant to open this conversation with Harry? She'd spent so much time while she'd been away looking forward to getting back and seeing him again. Now she was here, she felt at a total loss. He'd been a source of inspiration and excitement… and - dare she even admit it – hopes for the future. But now there was just this massive weight of dread that all of it was about to be whipped away from her.

Married?

Wife?

Cheater?

She could see Harry's Discovery ahead – pulled up right outside her garden gate. Well, it certainly looked like she was about to get her answers, didn't it?!

'Here's fine!' she said quickly.

'I can take you right to the gate!' said the drive, slowing down and glancing at her in the rear-view mirror.

'No – you'll be able to turn around much easier here with that other car down there!'

'Okay – you've got a point there,' he laughed.

'Thanks so much for the ride,' she said as she hauled herself out of the car. She handed him a wad of cash and a whopping tip, doing her best to focus on him instead of glancing over her shoulder and trying to get a glimpse of the man who'd just driven her to distraction for the past several hours.

'Let me get you some change,' said the driver, 'half a sec...'

'Oh no – no need. That's for you,' said Patricia, forcing herself to turn back to him and act like a vaguely normal human being for five more seconds.

'Well, that's very kind. Very kind indeed - thank you!' said the driver, beaming at her. 'Would you like a hand to shift this lot to your door?' he said, pointing at the pile of bags that he'd just placed on the bank – the lifejacket balanced jauntily on top. 'Don't want you floating away after all!' he added with a grin.

Patricia smiled back. 'No – thanks very much. I just need to nip around and... erm... check things in the garden before I go inside. After the rain. You know...'

The driver nodded. 'Well – you have a good day then.'

Patricia smiled again and waited impatiently while he got back in his car, then waved with relief as he turned it carefully around and disappeared from view.

The moment the rumble of the engine faded into the distance, Patricia felt a knot of nerves grab her by the throat. She'd hoped that the journey home would mean that she'd know what to say to Harry when she faced him – or at least that she'd be ready for this moment in some way. In reality, she just wasn't. She simply couldn't bear the idea that every wonderful thing she'd been imagining over the past few days might be about to disappear.

Well, there was nothing for it. She couldn't stand around here forever. Patricia turned and began marching towards her cottage, her eyes fixed on the ferry slip-way beyond.

There he was… exactly where she'd been imagining him the entire time she'd been away. Harry was busy with his back to her, standing next to the little ferry dock and knocking a wooden sign into the soft ground with a hammer.

As if he could sense someone watching him, Harry peeped over his shoulder. The minute he saw her walking towards him, his face split into a beautiful grin. It almost managed to stop her in her tracks. A tiny part of her brain begged her not to say anything and just bask in the warmth of his smile and his obvious delight at seeing her again.

'You're back!' he said, the pleasure on his face echoed perfectly in his voice, even as he kept hold of the post and hammer. 'How did it go?'

'Fine, thank you,' said Patricia. Her voice was cool, and the sensible part of her brain had clearly taken over again. 'You and I need to talk.'

Harry's eyes narrowed as he peered into her face. His expression flickered slightly – he could obviously tell that something wasn't right.

'Damn,' he said, his eyebrows raising. 'Am I in trouble again?'

'Maybe – maybe not,' said Patricia. 'I need to ask you a few questions... so it kind of depends on your answers.'

'O-kay,' said Harry tentatively, 'do you mind if I keep hammering though? I've just got this started and if I let go now it's going to fall over.'

Patricia shrugged. It wasn't quite the full, undivided attention that she'd been hoping for, but what other choice did she have?

Thump...

'I don't even know your surname,' said Patricia. Her voice sounded slightly desperate. What a weird place to start... but hey – at least she'd managed to say something.

Thump...

'That's easy enough... it's Lakin.'

Thump...

'Without an "r". Not Lar*king* or Lar*kin* – Harry Lakin.'

Thump...

Patricia nodded, trying to build up the courage to ask the important question.

'Are you married?' she blurted.

Thump! Thump! Thump!

It took a bit longer for Harry to pause and answer this one, which did absolutely nothing to calm Patricia's fear. Her heart seemed to be echoing his hammer strikes blow for blow.

'I was,' said Harry at last, 'once. Quite a long time

ago now. We're divorced. She's remarried and lives in a lovely house somewhere up north. I still get a birthday card – which is nice. Though I think it's because she likes to remind me how old I am!'

Harry took a breath and walloped the post a few more times.

'Are you seeing anyone else,' said Patricia, 'at the moment I mean?'

Harry stopped hammering and straightened the sign up a bit before turning to look at her fully. 'I thought I was – but currently, I'm not sure. Looks like the jury's out. I'll let you know in a few minutes.'

He turned back to the sign and carried on hammering, clearly happier now that he'd straightened it up.

Taking a moment to digest what Harry had just said, Patricia stared at the sign for something to do. It had been freshly painted and the lettering was beautifully done – expertly sign written in brightly coloured paint.

'Did you do that?' she asked distractedly.

'Yep,' said Harry, not pausing in what he was doing.

Patricia raised her eyebrows, impressed. Then another question pinged into her brain.

'What do you do for a living?'

'I'm retired,' said Harry.

'Rubbish,' said Patricia, 'you're too young to be retired.'

'Tell my ex-wife that,' said Harry with a chuckle.

'Answer the question!' snapped Patricia. She couldn't help it – all her senses were still on high alert.

'Okay, sorry,' laughed Harry, 'just trying to lighten the mood. I'm semi-retired. How's that?'

Patricia frowned in confusion, watching as Harry threw his hammer down into a beaten-up metal toolbox that was resting on the ground next to him.

'So what did you used to do?' she asked curiously.

'I had a business repairing and restoring old bicycles,' said Harry.

Patricia's thoughts flew to poor old Wally - rusting away in the shed because she couldn't bear to be parted with him, even though he was most definitely done-for without professional help.

'You're joking?' she said as a smile began to tug at the corner of her lips.

Much to her surprise, there was suddenly a defiant jut to Harry's chin and he crossed his arms defensively across his chest.

'Not everyone understands,' he said, clearly misunderstanding her reply. 'They've got nice wide saddles – sit up and beg handlebars with proper bells on them - and none of those tricky gear-levers like your bike's got. I like the ones with proper old chains and lousy brakes.'

'I didn't mean-' Patricia held up her hands in a gesture of apology, but Harry was clearly not done with his rant just yet.

'I'm used to people not getting it,' he sighed. 'It's

exactly why I handed the workshop over to James. He wanted to specialise in those horrid new things. He'll do really well too, no doubt, when he gets back to it. He likes all that modern nonsense. Me? I like nothing better than spending a whole day remodelling a wicker basket for a customer. James thinks I'm a dinosaur, though. He reckons it's more efficient just to buy in everything you need – plastic baskets - stickers instead of hand-painted – whatever next? Anyway – we just had to agree to disagree in the end,' he finished with a huff.

'I'm on your side,' said Patricia, smiling at him. His rant about something that was clearly so important to him made her think of her own horror at losing her beloved vintage knitting patterns. No one else had really understood that either. Harry would though, wouldn't he? And Wally… he'd certainly understand about Wally…

'Sure you are,' said Harry, smiling at her ruefully. 'I can't imagine that with the posh new jobbie you were riding when we first met!'

'I'd hardly call that riding!' laughed Patricia. 'No, seriously – I *hate* that bike. It's new and…' she suddenly moved forward, grabbed his hand and gave it a tug. 'Come with me a sec!'

Harry looked at her in complete confusion, but with a small smile playing on his lips, he let Patricia tow him back up towards her garden gate.

Patricia had to restrain herself from jumping on

Harry as he threaded his fingers through hers – but she wanted him to see – wanted him to realise that she really, truly *did* understand him.

She drew to a halt in front of her little lean-to shed at the side of the cottage, and reluctantly she dropped his warm, rough hand. Sliding the heavy bolt back, she yanked open the wooden door with its peeling green paint.

'There,' she said triumphantly, beckoning Harry forward, 'take a look. There's someone I want you to meet…'

'You keep someone locked up in your shed?!' Harry let out a slightly nervous laugh but stepped forwards anyway.

'You won't be able to miss him, I promise!'

Harry peered tentatively into the gloom.

'Harry, meet Wally,' she said with a grin.

'Wow! What a lovely chap!' said Harry. 'Someone needs some TLC!'

'He definitely needs some work,' said Patricia, unable to keep the ridiculous smile off her face. 'I rode him everywhere until a few weeks ago… but I couldn't bring myself to get rid of him.'

'I should think not!' said Harry seriously, moving into the cobwebby space and running a tender hand over Wally's rusty handlebars.

'See – told you I was on your side,' said Patricia, smiling as she watched Harry checking Wally over like he was a lame horse.

'So you are,' said Harry, his voice full of wonder. 'Would you like me to have a look at him now? We could bring him out onto the bank for a bit more light?'

Patricia thought about it for a second... a very *very* short second, and then she shook her head. Stepping into the shed, she reached for Harry's hand again.

He turned to her, his face creasing in a warm, slow smile as she reached up and brushed a cobweb from his hair. Even in the gloom, his hazel and emerald eyes held her captivated.

'Maybe later?' she breathed, her arms wrapping around his waist as she pulled him close.

Harry nodded and went to speak, but he couldn't get the words out because Patricia's lips were already on his.

THE END

ALSO BY BETH RAIN

Little Bamton Series:

Little Bamton: The Complete Series Collection: Books 1 - 5

Individual titles:

Christmas Lights and Snowball Fights (Little Bamton Book 1)

Spring Flowers and April Showers (Little Bamton Book 2)

Summer Nights and Pillow Fights (Little Bamton Book 3)

Autumn Cuddles and Muddy Puddles (Little Bamton Book 4)

Christmas Flings and Wedding Rings (Little Bamton Book 5)

Upper Bamton Series:

A New Arrival in Upper Bamton (Upper Bamton Book 1)

Rainy Days in Upper Bamton (Upper Bamton Book 2)

Hidden Treasures in Upper Bamton (Upper Bamton Book 3)

Time Flies By in Upper Bamton (Upper Bamton Book 4)

Standalone Books:

Christmas on Crumcarey

Seabury Series:

Welcome to Seabury (Seabury Book 1)

Trouble in Seabury (Seabury Book 2)

Christmas in Seabury (Seabury Book 3)

Sandwiches in Seabury (Seabury Book 4)

Secrets in Seabury (Seabury Book 5)

Surprises in Seabury (Seabury Book 6)

Dreams and Ice Creams in Seabury (Seabury Book 7)

Mistakes and Heartbreaks in Seabury (Seabury Book 8)

Laughter and Happy Ever After in Seabury (Seabury Book 9)

Seabury Series Collections:

Kate's Story: Books 1 - 3

Hattie's Story: Books 4 - 6

Writing as Bea Fox:

What's a Girl To Do? The Complete Series

Individual titles:

The Holiday: What's a Girl To Do? (Book 1)

The Wedding: What's a Girl To Do? (Book 2)

The Lookalike: What's a Girl To Do? (Book 3)

The Reunion: What's a Girl To Do? (Book 4)

At Christmas: What's a Girl To Do? (Book 5)

ABOUT THE AUTHOR

Beth Rain has always wanted to be a writer and has been penning adventures for characters ever since she learned to stare into the middle-distance and daydream.

She currently lives in the (sometimes) sunny South West, and it is a dream come true to spend her days hanging out with Bob – her trusty laptop – scoffing crisps and chocolate while dreaming up swoony love stories for all her imaginary friends.

Beth's writing will always deliver on the happy-ever-afters, so if you need cosy… you're in safe hands!

Visit www.bethrain.com for all the bookish goodness and keep up with all Beth's news by joining her monthly newsletter!

facebook.com/BethRainBooks
twitter.com/bethrainauthor
instagram.com/bethrainauthor